**"Don't move. We only want her."** The masked man pointed the barrel of his gun in Kaylin's direction.

Hudson kept his hand on the Smith & Wesson still holstered at his hip. "Who are you and what do you want with Kaylin?"

"None of your concern, Constable. Take your hand off that gun of yours."

Hudson lifted his hands in surrender but inched closer to one of the assailants. "Tell us what you want."

A sneer peeked out from behind the man's mask. "I told you. He wants her."

"He?"

"The boss."

Could he mean Valentino? "Look, you don't have to do this. Surrender and we'll take that into–"

The mansion's front door opened.

It was enough of a distraction to act. Both Kaylin and Hudson whipped out their weapons, crouching behind the back of the cruiser.

Hudson turned back to the gunman. "Give it up, man. You won't get away with this."

But the silent masked man fired in their direction, bullets spraying the area.

W9-BUA-587

**Darlene L. Turner** is an award-winning author who lives with her husband, Jeff, in Ontario, Canada. Her love of suspense began when she read her first Nancy Drew book. She's turned that passion into her writing and believes readers will be captured by her plots, inspired by her strong characters and moved by her inspirational message. Visit Darlene at www.darlenelturner.com, where there's suspense beyond borders.

### Books by Darlene L. Turner

### Love Inspired Suspense

*Border Breach*

# BORDER BREACH

# DARLENE L. TURNER

**LOVE INSPIRED** SUSPENSE
INSPIRATIONAL ROMANCE

If you purchased this book without a cover you should be aware that this book is stolen property. It was reported as "unsold and destroyed" to the publisher, and neither the author nor the publisher has received any payment for this "stripped book."

# LOVE INSPIRED® SUSPENSE
## INSPIRATIONAL ROMANCE

Recycling programs
for this product may
not exist in your area.

ISBN-13: 978-1-335-40277-6

Border Breach

Copyright © 2020 by Darlene L. Turner

All rights reserved. No part of this book may be used or reproduced in any manner whatsoever without written permission except in the case of brief quotations embodied in critical articles and reviews.

This is a work of fiction. Names, characters, places and incidents are either the product of the author's imagination or are used fictitiously. Any resemblance to actual persons, living or dead, businesses, companies, events or locales is entirely coincidental.

This edition published by arrangement with Harlequin Books S.A.

For questions and comments about the quality of this book, please contact us at CustomerService@Harlequin.com.

Love Inspired
22 Adelaide St. West, 40th Floor
Toronto, Ontario M5H 4E3, Canada
www.Harlequin.com

Printed in U.S.A.

Forbearing one another, and forgiving one another,
if any man have a quarrel against any:
even as Christ forgave you, so also do ye.
–*Colossians* 3:13

For Jeff, my forever love.

# ONE

Officer Kaylin Poirier's stomach lurched at the sight of the two people inside a white florist van that pulled up to her booth at the Windsor-Detroit border. The driver wouldn't meet her gaze and his passenger couldn't sit still. Their body language elevated her guard. Could it simply be her overactive imagination or perhaps the humid weather putting her in a foul mood? Experience said there was more to it. This was her job, to protect the border and catch criminals illegally importing goods into Canada—whether it be drugs, weapons or immigrants. Today was no different.

Actually, today *was* different. Security at the border had been tightened by her father, Chief of Police Marshall Poirier. "We will find every drug smuggler and stop them before they can enter Canada. My daughter will make sure of it," he'd said at a joint television press conference earlier in the morning.

She winced at the memory of his firm grip on her arm and commanding voice as he spoke. He'd vowed to clear his city of drugs after numerous gangs had terrorized the community with deadly narcotics. Too many teens had died in the past two months.

And he expected her to get the job done.

*No pressure.*

She wiped perspiration off her forehead and extended her hand out the window of the booth. "Passports, please."

She eyed the inside of the van, checking for contents, but

rear of the vehicle was hidden by a partition. Not good. She would have to go around and open the back doors.

The men handed over their passports, and she ran them through the bar scanner. "How long were you in the States?"

"One day." The driver wiped his brow, chewing on his lip.

The passenger tugged at his hoodie and sat further back into his seat.

Kaylin checked her computer, noting their nervousness. Strange. "What are you declaring?"

"Flowers, ma'am." The driver produced a paper. "Here's the phytosanitary certificate allowing us to bring them into the country."

She examined the document to determine if all the correct signatures and details were included. Satisfied it was legit, she passed it back to him.

He took the form with a shaky hand.

Detector Dog Services Officer Nolan Keene walked in front of her booth with one of their dogs. The DDS worked with the Canada Border Services Agency and patrolled the border frequently, checking for smuggled goods. The older man had mentored Kaylin during her probation period two years ago and now often shared advice with her on what to observe when inspecting cars as they traveled over the border.

The beagle stopped and growled at the van, inching its way toward the vehicle.

Kaylin's muscles tensed. Something was up. The dog's actions confirmed her suspicions that she needed to investigate this van more closely. No way would she let the men pass without further inspection, especially with her father counting on her.

She stepped outside her booth and stood in front of the

driver's window. "Sir, can you shut off the vehicle and give me your keys?" She held out her left hand, keeping her right positioned on her weapon.

He shifted in his seat, exposing a gun in his lap. He fingered his Glock. A picture of Kaylin and her father at the press conference lay on top of the middle console.

Kaylin's pulse palpitated, throbbing in her head. Why would they have her picture? Her training kicked in and she whipped out her 9 mm as she stepped an inch to the right to get out of his line of fire. "Gun! Hand it over. Now."

The driver's expression turned to a daring snare.

Nolan pulled his weapon from his holster. The beagle barked, tugging the officer toward the commotion.

The rows of cars lined up to cross the border reminded Kaylin of the pending danger. She needed to contain the situation before panic set in and others got hurt. She wouldn't allow that on her watch.

The man opened his door in a flash, shoving Kaylin to the ground. Then he aimed his gun on her.

Before he could act, Kaylin rolled to the back of the van and crouched in an attack position. She pressed her radio button. "Officer in need of assistance. Hostiles armed and dangerous. Booth two."

Nolan took cover behind a column and pointed his gun toward the vehicle. The beagle continued to bark, intent on protecting those around him.

The driver pulled the door shut, fired a shot out the window and gunned the engine, tires squealing on the concrete.

"Oh no, you don't." Kaylin fired.

She hit the driver's-side mirror, causing the vehicle to swerve for a split second. The driver straightened the van and stepped on the gas.

He shot back, the bullet slamming into the concrete

beside Kaylin. She scrambled to her booth, taking a position behind the wall, her heart jackknifing to her throat.

Nolan returned fire, damaging the rear window.

Sirens sounded as CBSA vehicles made their way to Kaylin's booth. They pulled in front of the van, blocking its path.

The driver increased his speed and swerved around the vehicles, scraping the side of the concrete barrier. Then the van raced off into the distance.

Kaylin mumbled under her breath and holstered her weapon. Her fellow officers radioed ahead to the local Ontario Provincial Police to pursue the suspects. OPP patrolled the highways and would be nearby. Hopefully they'd intercept the fleeing van and stop it from getting further inside the Canadian border. Kaylin hated that the two men in the van had gotten away. Not a good start to tightening security at her border.

Other CBSA officers directed the bottleneck of cars to the remaining booths. They needed to keep them moving.

Nolan approached Kaylin with the dog. "You okay?"

She brushed gravel off her uniform. "Perturbed they escaped." Tightness grabbed her chest, reminding her of her father's impending wrath for not doing a thorough job. No doubt she would hear from him and her boss.

"Agreed. Time for the OPP to take over." He petted the dog. "Duke sure had a nose for something in that van."

"Good boy." She rubbed the beagle's head. "I wonder what they were smuggling." And what was their intent with her?

Duke barked. Nolan ruffled the dog's ears. "Let's hope we catch them and find out."

Kaylin's radio crackled. "Officer Poirier, this is Dispatch," the female said. "Be advised the police are en route to your location to discuss the incident."

She stiffened. Great. Now she had to report to the police on the situation.

The last time she had to work with them did not go well.

A police cruiser pulled up at her booth and an officer stepped out.

Kaylin sucked in a breath.

*Not him again.*

Canadian police constable Hudson Steeves adjusted the holster at his waist and made his way over to the border patrol officer he needed to interview. The one involved with this morning's incident with the florist van. Not a coincidence the altercation had happened shortly after they received a tip of the doda drug being smuggled into Canada via this exact border.

That was why he was here. To determine whether the driver of the van brought doda into their country. He was now part of a joint task force the chief of police had assembled.

Plus, he had made a promise to his sister to catch the drug ring that had targeted his nephew.

He stopped when he saw the CBSA officer standing near her booth.

Chief Marshall Poirier's daughter.

Kaylin Poirier was the most stubborn woman he'd ever met. Sure, he noted how the tall brunette stood with her hands on her hips, looking more beautiful than when he'd seen her six months ago. However, he would not get sucker punched by a woman again.

*Focus.*

He tipped his hat at the two officers. "Morning."

Kaylin crossed her arms. "Constable Steeves, what brings you here?" Her question held a curtness to it.

Images of their last case together flashed before him.

Things had not gone smoothly: they'd almost lost their suspect because of their constant bickering, and he had nearly been fired. He'd vowed never to let it happen again during an investigation.

He squinted in the June sunlight. "The incident with the florist van."

A wrinkle distorted her brow as she averted her gaze. "It occurred ten minutes ago. How did you get here so fast?"

Her body language told him she was annoyed by his presence.

Hudson eyed the other officer and extended his hand. "Constable Hudson Steeves. You are?"

"Nolan Keene with Detector Dog Services for the CBSA." They shook hands. Nolan held up his dog's leash. "This is Duke."

Hudson nodded. "Nice to meet you both." He turned back to Kaylin. "To answer your question, we had an anonymous tip that a shipment of a drug named doda was coming across the border. I was on my way over here when I heard the call about the chase."

Kaylin adjusted the radio on her shoulder. "I don't have an update for you. The OPP are still in pursuit."

He took a step forward. "You hurt? I heard they shot at a CBSA officer."

She tightened her arm muscles. "I'm fine. Nothing I can't handle."

Nolan motioned for Duke to sit. "How do you two know each other?"

"We worked on a case together six months ago," Kaylin said.

Hudson pulled out a notebook. "Tell me about this van. What did the driver look like?"

"Asian. Approximately twenty-five. The passenger was

wearing a hoodie, so I couldn't see his face clearly." Kaylin shook her head.

Hudson positioned his pen. "What happened?"

"I became suspicious as soon as their van pulled up to my booth."

"Why?"

"Tense body language," Kaylin said. "And then when Nolan and Duke walked by, Duke growled."

Nolan rubbed the beagle's ears. "One of his signs that he smelled something inside that van."

Kaylin eyed the dog and nodded. "I stepped out of my booth and up to the driver's window, requesting he turn off the engine and hand me the keys. Then I saw the gun."

"You're fortunate you didn't get hurt. What happened next?"

She kicked a stone and dragged the toe of her boot in a circle.

She was stalling. Obviously, something bothered her.

He took a step closer. "What is it?"

She shoved her hands in her pockets. "They had a picture of me and my dad at the press conference this morning." A pause. "Why would they have that?"

*What?* Not what he was expecting her to say. "They targeted you?"

"How would they know which booth I was at?"

Hudson glanced around. "They're watching you. Are you normally at this one?"

"Mostly, but not always." Duke nudged her hand, licking it. She looked down at the dog. "You know how to lighten the mood, don't you, boy?" She squatted and rubbed the dog's neck.

"How did you get away?" Hudson asked.

"I scrambled out of their line of fire. That was when

Nolan ran toward us. It startled them and they pulled away. I shot at the van. Didn't stop them, though."

"We radioed the OPP to pursue them," Nolan said. "That's the last we heard."

"Police joined in on the chase just as I arrived here." We often work together with the OPP and other law enforcements on joint task forces.

Nolan adjusted the dog's collar and Duke wagged his tail. "Well, I gotta get this guy back to work. Nice meeting you, Constable." With a wave, Nolan spun on his heels and left.

"Let's check the area for shell casings." Hudson tucked his notebook back in his front shirt pocket.

"We should find mine, Nolan's and the driver's." Kaylin scoured around her booth as the other CBSA officers directed the lines of cars through the border.

Hudson pointed to the shiny casing glittering in the sunlight. He put gloves on and picked it up. "This yours?"

She peered closer. "9 mm. Looks like it."

He inspected the booth's doorway and found two 10 mm casings. "Gotcha." He bagged them and tucked it into his pocket. "Let me see if I can get an update." He punched in his sergeant's number. "Hey, Sarge, any word on the pursuit at the border with the OPP?"

"They found the van abandoned and on fire. Footprints appeared in the dirt. The driver and passenger must have fled through the woods."

"Any goods found at the scene?" He turned for privacy.

"That's what you need to find out. I'll text you the address. Survey the area. I spoke with the CBSA officials and looks like you'll be working with the chief's daughter, Kaylin, on this task force. Know her?"

He tightened his grip on his phone and a lump formed in his throat. Could he work with her again?

A horn honked in the distance. The booths were filled with cars bumper to bumper. Another busy day at the border with thousands of passengers wanting to either visit or reenter their normally peaceful country. Too bad this day had been tainted with scandal.

"Talking with her right now." He turned back to face her and caught his breath. Maybe he could make amends for the last time.

Kaylin's eyebrows rose.

"Get this going. I'm counting on you to catch this drug gang. We need to stop it before it continues to hit the streets." Sergeant Peter Miller clicked off the call.

Hudson stuffed his cell phone in his pocket. "Looks like we'll be working together again."

Her face contorted. "What are you talking about?"

"We're looking into the uprise of the doda drug and I've joined the task force to stop the smugglers. Get your gear."

She fisted her hands on her hips, eyes turning cold. "I'm working a lane today." Her cell phone buzzed. She pulled it out of her pocket and checked the screen. She grimaced as the text message confirmed her earlier suspicions. "My father heard about today's incident. Great. I'll never hear the end of this."

Her clipped tone spoke of possible friction between father and daughter. Would it cause problems? "They found the van abandoned. We need to go check it out. See what evidence we can find," Hudson said.

"I can't leave in the middle of a shift. My boss wouldn't—"

Bullets ricocheted off the pavement.

They were under fire.

# TWO

Hudson threw himself on top of Kaylin, pushing her into the booth to take cover. "You okay?"

"Not hit."

He ignored his galloping heartbeat, whipped out his Smith & Wesson and aimed it through the entrance.

Where was the shooter? Were they targeting Kaylin? Muffled screams echoed throughout the stalled lanes of traffic.

Another round of bullets hit the booth, penetrating the glass and creating a spiderweb effect on the window. Several shards bit into his arm and blood began to ooze from the cuts instantly. He winced but dismissed the pain and dared a glance into the parking lot.

Gunfire peppered a nearby car's windshield. He needed to check on the occupants.

"Where's the shooter?" Kaylin stayed low and pointed her weapon out the broken window.

"No idea, but there can't be too many places for the sniper to hide. Obviously, someone knows what they're doing." He took out his phone and punched 911, relaying their location and the number of shots fired.

Pounding footsteps sounded nearby as more CBSA officers made their way to the area.

Hudson waved at them. "Stay down!"

After several minutes of silence, Hudson slipped his gun back in its holster. He and Kaylin eased out of the booth, feet crunching on the broken glass.

"You hurt?" His gaze caught hers and held.

She hesitated. "I'm good. What about the other drivers, though?"

Hudson nodded and ran to the car hit by bullets to ensure they didn't have any victims. He approached the vehicle with caution.

The couple lay on the front seat, shielding their heads.

Hudson opened the door. "Everyone okay?"

They peeked up, brushing off shards of glass. "They didn't hit us. Just the windshield."

Did this shooting have anything to do with the earlier incident? Were the suspects really targeting Kaylin and had they come back to finish the job?

Sirens pierced the area. EMS and local authorities weaved through the lanes. Windsor police officers piled out of their cruisers and approached them for a briefing on the situation.

After an intensive search of the area, Kaylin holstered her 9 mm. "Shooter is gone."

Hudson wiped the perspiration from his forehead. The June morning had already turned muggy. "Sniper fired multiple shots. Hit the booth and a car," he informed the Windsor police officers.

Hudson eyed Kaylin's rigid body. Just like him, she stood on guard for more shots, but the bags under her eyes didn't have anything to do with the tension from the shooting. They revealed sleep deprivation. Why? The pretty officer was stressed about something in her life and he had the sudden urge to find out what it was. To help.

Officers moved to examine the booth, combing the area for shell casings, while a paramedic bandaged Hudson's arm.

"Kaylin." Another CBSA officer headed in their direction. "Need to speak with you."

She groaned. "Here he comes."

"Who?" Hudson squinted to get a better look at the older gentleman.

"My boss. Probably wants to give me an earful for not manning my post efficiently. He seems to have it in for me."

The Goliath-like officer stepped forward. "Everyone okay?"

"Yes." She shoved her hands into her pockets. "What's going on?"

He pointed to Hudson as he spoke to her. "You've been reassigned from duty here to work with Constable Steeves on a task force your father has created. You now take orders from the constable."

Hudson grimaced. How would she react to the chain of command? The last time they'd worked together, she'd had a hard time taking orders from him.

"What about the shooting?" She pointed to the booth.

"We'll leave that to the local authorities. You're to work with your father and the police in busting this ring. I'm counting on you to do a good job. You hear?"

Her eyes narrowed and she scowled. "Yes, sir. You can expect nothing but my best. As always." She folded her arms across her chest, revealing her foul mood.

What had happened for her to get her back up so easily with her boss? Something in their past, or was she known for not doing her job effectively?

Hudson cleared his throat. "Thanks for your help, sir. You can count on us wrapping this up as quickly as possible. I'm sure Officer Poirier is needed back on the team." He turned to Kaylin and pointed to the officers scouring the area. "Let's leave this shooting with them and go check out the florist van. Forensics are en route."

"Whatever you say, Constable." She flattened her lips.

Great. Not only did he have to deal with a shooting today, but an angry female, as well.

Not a good combination.

Kaylin jumped into the constable's vehicle and slammed the door. Why did she have to work with him again? When they'd worked together last time, he'd taken over the case, pushing her aside so he could fly solo. He had a problem with authority and only wanted to do things his way. She folded her arms and stared out the window.

Didn't matter that Hudson Steeves was one of the best-looking men she'd ever met. Those cornflower blue eyes were hard not to get lost in, but she was determined not to get sucked into another man's good looks. Jake, her ex-fiancé, was incentive enough to steer her away from all men. His tricks had taken the ultimate toll and there was no way she'd open herself up to that kind of pain again.

Hudson pulled onto the highway that would take them to the charred van. "It's good to be working with you again," he said, spouting the professional line. "How have you been?"

Despite her resolve to stay close-minded toward him, she snuck a peek at his side profile. His chiseled jaw, covered by a five o'clock shadow, made him even more handsome. *Stop, Kaylin.* She turned back to the window. The tree line zipped by as they moved in and out of the busy traffic. "Working nonstop," she replied. "You?" She was working hard, but mostly so she didn't have time to think about being alone. After all, her experience with the men in her life proved she was better off by herself. Although, if that was the case, why did she have to keep reminding herself of that?

"The same," he said. "Never a dull moment."

"For sure. Tell me about this case. How did you stumble onto it?"

He took the next right and maneuvered the cruiser into

the heart of downtown Windsor. "Doda—the poor man's heroin street drug—has been on the rise again. The police staged a siege with the CBSA in Saskatchewan a few weeks ago. Unfortunately, the arrest didn't include the big cheese of the operation. Just a few men from lower on the totem pole. Ever since then we've gotten reports of the drug being used in different cities. Toronto's Asian community seems to be the hardest hit."

"Interesting that the driver was Asian. Any connection?"

"Possibly."

"Are they targeting a specific ethnic group?" She plunged herself into getting more information on the case. Anything to direct her away from thoughts of the handsome constable.

"It used to be mostly in the Asian community, but we're finding more high school and college kids are starting to use the drug." His knuckles whitened as he tightened his grip on the steering wheel. "We have to stop it before it gets any worse."

"I've heard it's a hard drug to kick."

"Yes, that's true, especially without the help of a doctor."

Kaylin shook her head. Just the thought of kids taking this drug put her on edge. "When will people learn drugs are not the answer?" Images of her brother popped in her head. She wrung her hands together. She knew firsthand what it was like to have drugs take over a loved one's life. She had watched it happen bit by bit with her brother.

"You okay?" Hudson's eyes softened.

Had he changed since they'd last worked together? Interest in him tugged at her emotions, but she turned away to block out his boyish charm. "My brother overdosed on heroin at the age of eighteen, so drugs have always been a sore spot for me."

"I'm so sorry. How old were you?"

She let out a heavy sigh. "Ten at the time, but I can still picture his lifeless eyes."

"You found him?"

Tears welled, but she pushed them away. She would not let him see her in a weakened state. "Yes, and my father blamed me for it."

He pulled into the parking lot of an abandoned warehouse. "The police chief? That's terrible. How could he have done that?"

"Let's just say my father blames me for a lot of things." That was more than she wanted to share. The memories were all in her past and she had to keep them there. For her own sanity.

"Well, it could hardly be your fault. What did your mother say?"

She stared out the window. "She died giving birth to me, so I never knew her. Another thing my father hated me for."

"Doesn't sound like the man I've met."

Her father put on a good image for the public, but she knew his secret. Who he really was. "No comment." She rubbed her temples. She needed to change the subject. "How did you get chosen for this task force?"

A vein twitched in his neck as he jerked the car to the right, where she saw the remains of the charred van. "I asked to be on it."

"Why?"

"Personal reasons."

He wasn't offering much information. Why the secret, she wondered. "Like?" She continued to push.

"My nephew Matthew overdosed after he was targeted by a drug ring. He's in the hospital."

"I'm so sorry." Once again, Todd's face flashed before her. She could relate to Hudson's pain.

"I'm determined to stop drug smugglers. I've seen what

it can do to teens. It has to end." His taut expression revealed just how much he wanted to catch them.

Her cell phone dinged. She pulled it out and read the text.

Next time you won't be so fortunate. We're watching.

A picture popped on her phone. One of her and Hudson standing near her booth at the border.

She swallowed despite her dry mouth. Yes, she agreed with Hudson. These smugglers had to be stopped or someone could be hurt. Or worse.

"What is it?" Hudson parked beside another cruiser and turned off the engine.

"Got a text and this." She held up the picture on her phone. "They're watching."

His eyes narrowed. "This is not good. How did they get your number?"

"No idea." A tremor rippled through her body, threatening to overpower her. She forced it away and shoved her cell phone into her vest pocket.

"You best report it." Hudson grabbed gloves from a bag in the back seat and handed her a pair. "Let's see if we can salvage anything from this wreckage."

Kaylin put them on and stepped out of the vehicle. Smoke assaulted her nostrils and she pinched her nose. Firemen had doused the van's smoldering embers. Only a charred shell remained.

"I doubt we'll find much." Kaylin stepped forward. "Why do you think they did this?"

"I'm guessing they knew we'd catch up to them at some point, so they decided to get rid of any evidence." He turned toward another officer at the scene. "James, did we get any leads on what direction they went? It can't be far."

The white-haired constable shook his head. "We have

officers canvassing the area, but so far it's like they disappeared."

"Always one step ahead." Hudson rubbed the back of his neck.

A lone remaining fireman approached the group. "The flames are out and it's safe to search the van. It's all yours now."

Hudson touched Kaylin gently by the elbow, guiding her toward the vehicle. "We need to wait for our Ident team."

She trembled at his innocent touch.

They didn't have long to wait. The forensic unit pulled into the parking lot and two officers rushed forward with their equipment. Another cruiser pulled up beside them and a female constable emerged.

Hudson approached her and held out his hand. "Hey, Bianca. Good to see you again."

She pointed to the van. "Have you contaminated the crime scene?"

"Wouldn't think of it," Hudson said. "This is Kaylin Poirier, CBSA officer. She's here to help with the investigation. Kaylin, this is Constable Bianca Wills. She works alongside the forensic team and reports back to us."

"Nice to meet you." Bianca motioned toward the van. "Shall we take a look?"

Hudson put his gloves on and opened the back doors. The hinges screeched in annoyance.

Kaylin peered closer.

Empty, charred tin plant buckets lay on the floor.

Kaylin pointed to a pot. "What? They torched the van because of flowers? That doesn't make sense."

"They had to be some form of illegal flower." Hudson moved to the front of the vehicle. "Let's check out the seat."

Kaylin opened what was left of the driver's door. Searching cars was part of a CBSA officer's duty. She could do this. It was her comfort zone. "Do you mind if I take a look here?"

"Go ahead," Bianca replied. "Just don't move anything."

Kaylin reached in and felt around the seats. Nothing. She placed her hand behind the blackened cushion. Something pricked her finger and she snapped back. "I think there's a knife in here."

Bianca reached in and pulled out a blade.

Kaylin leaned closer. "I imagine the fire removed any chances of getting a print off it."

"Probably, but we'll check to be sure." Bianca dropped the knife into an evidence bag and handed it to the forensics officer.

Kaylin ran her hand along the inside of the door. "Nothing hidden there. Looks like they kept a clean van."

Hudson handed Bianca a card. "Can you call me when you hear anything?"

"Sure will."

"See ya around." Hudson's cell phone buzzed. He fished it out of his pocket and swiped the screen.

Kaylin kept her gaze on Hudson. His presence lured her in like a lobster to a trap, ensnaring her so she couldn't escape.

Hudson's expression clouded as he read the text. "We gotta roll."

"What's going on?" She removed her gloves.

"A suspicious package was found at my nephew's high school. Could be related to the case."

The hairs prickled the back of her neck.

What else would this day bring?

# THREE

Hudson took the steps two at a time into Matthew's high school with Kaylin at his heels. He needed to get to the bottom of this doda ring, and fast. Before more kids were enticed. His nephew's safety depended on it. Lockers lined each side of the sparse halls as their footsteps echoed down the corridor. It was lunchtime, so the halls were empty of students.

He pointed to the right. "The principal's office is this way."

"You've been here before, I take it?" She grinned.

He stopped, her sassy smile tantalizing him. *Wait. What? Where did that come from?* She probably still hated him. Not that he blamed her. He'd acted like a jerk on their previous investigation. He'd broken up with his fiancée and was still getting over her betrayal. Rebecca had brought out the worst in him. And Kaylin had paid the price. He'd ended up praying a lot during that time—asking God to forgive him.

*Focus on the case.*

"Yup, my old high school."

When they reached the office, Hudson knocked on the door and stepped aside, letting Kaylin enter first. Her floral scent followed and he breathed it in. He adjusted his hat to help him concentrate on the task at hand.

A woman in her late forties sat behind a desk, typing. Piles of paperwork filled the top of her working area. She sipped her drink and glanced up at the interruption.

Hudson pulled out his credentials. "Good afternoon, ma'am. I'm Constable Hudson Steeves." He pointed to Kaylin. "This is Officer Kaylin Poirier of the CBSA."

The secretary stood, her glasses slipping to the end of her nose. Her raised brows peeked over her cat-eye spectacles. "You're here about the drugs, aren't you?"

Hudson put his badge in his pocket. "Yes. Can we talk to Principal Normand?"

She picked up the phone and buzzed into the inner office. "The officers are here about the package." She paused. "Will do." She pointed to the door. "You can go in. He's expecting you."

Hudson and Kaylin entered the small office lined with bookshelves on both sides.

The silver-haired man stood. "Good afternoon, Officers. Thanks for coming."

Hudson stuck out his hand and introduced himself and Kaylin.

"Nice to meet you both." The principal came out from behind his desk and returned the gesture before pointing to the table. "Here's the package in question. We received a tip that someone had brought drugs into the school, so we did a locker-by-locker search and found this."

Hudson opened the bag and sniffed the beige powder. He stuck his finger in and scooped up a trace with his pinkie. "It's doda all right. Where's the student? We'd like to talk to him."

"He's being detained down the hall by another teacher. His father is also there. He's madder than a stirred-up hornet's nest."

Hudson pulled out a folded evidence bag from his pocket, placed the doda into it and sealed the top. "We'll take this to the station for processing." He pointed to the door. "Lead us to the student."

Hudson turned to exit the room and bumped into Kaylin, almost knocking her over. He caught her by the waist as their gaze locked. He cleared his throat and stepped aside. "After you."

They followed Principal Normand down the hall to a classroom. A curly-haired teenager slouched in the chair behind a desk. The teacher sat at the front of the room. A sophisticated gentleman in an Armani suit stood in the corner with his arms crossed. He looked at his watch before peering at them with a scowl.

It was evident they were taking up the man's valuable time.

Hudson knew the type. A father who needed complete control of his kids.

Principal Normand pointed toward them. "Benji, these officers are here to talk to you. I suggest you cooperate. You're already under suspension. Don't make me kick you out of school."

The father rushed forward, standing toe-to-toe with the principal. "You wouldn't dare. My son will not be treated this way."

Hudson stepped between them and extended his hand. "I'm Constable Steeves. You are?"

"David Rossiter." He kept his arms glued to his side. "Constable, you better be careful on how you treat this situation or I won't hesitate to sue your department."

Great. If that happened, he'd never hear the end of it from his boss. And it'd be just what he needed. Another strike against him. "We want to get to the bottom of what happened here, sir. I hope you will cooperate."

The man said nothing; he just stared at Hudson, whose own gaze didn't waver.

Then, finally, David Rossiter stood aside.

Hudson pulled up a chair next to the boy and straddled it. He held up the bag. "Benji, is this yours?"

"Nope."

"Why was it found in your locker?"

The boy shrugged.

Kaylin stepped closer and stood in the boy's personal space. "Be honest with us and we may let you off easy. Where did you get the doda?"

Hudson waited for a response, but the boy said nothing.

The teacher stood. "Benji, cooperate with them."

Silence filled the stuffy room. The teen studied the floor, remaining mute.

"Come on, Benji, give us something. We want the dealer." Hudson's cell phone played his sister's ringtone. He stood. "I need to take this."

As soon as he stepped into the hall, he asked, "Ally, what's wrong?" She didn't normally call during his work shift. Something had happened.

She sniffed. "Matty has slipped into a coma." Her voice quivered.

He stiffened and gripped his phone tighter. "I'm so sorry, sweetie."

"Find the monsters who did this to my boy."

Ally hadn't believed her son had taken the overdose. She'd insisted he'd been forced. But she couldn't say why. "I will. I'm working on a lead right now. I promise I'll find them." Could he really? *Lord, make it so.* "Keep me updated. Love you."

"You, too." She clicked off.

Hudson rammed his phone back into his pocket and stormed through the classroom door. "Do you know Matthew Wilson?" he shouted at Benji.

David rushed to his son's side. "Lay off, Constable, or I will talk to your superiors." His icy tone revealed he meant business.

Hudson didn't flinch and kept his gaze on the teen. He

wouldn't let this father get in the way of the investigation. "I repeat. Do you know Matthew Wilson?"

Benji met his gaze. "Yes. Why?"

"He's in a coma thanks to a drug overdose. Do you know what's special about this version of doda?"

"He'll kill me," Benji whispered.

"What? Who will kill you? What are you talking about?"

David put a hand on Benji's shoulder. "Son, be careful what you say."

Benji recoiled from his father's touch. "He told me if I said anything he would come after me and my family. You know, like this." He motioned a knife being slid across his neck.

"We can protect you. We just want this drug off the streets." Hudson pulled a notebook from his pocket. "Tell us what you know."

"I don't know his name. Only how to get in touch with them."

"How?" Kaylin asked.

Benji bit his fingernails. "I text a number. They tell me where to meet."

Kaylin sat at the desk next to the teenager. "So, you know what he looks like?"

"It's a different person each time."

Hudson frowned. The drug dealer used his thugs to make the drop in order to conceal his identity. How far did this ring spread?

He knew what he had to do. It was their best shot to get the dealer out of hiding. "Let's text the number, shall we? Tell them you need more drugs and you'll only meet at the school parking lot at six tonight."

The boy shook his head. "They won't go for that."

"Try it. What do you have to lose?"

Benji rubbed his temples. "My life."

David Rossiter slammed his hand on the desk. "You will not put my son's life at risk. I forbid it."

Kaylin leaned forward. "We'll protect him. Put a wire on him."

The man leaned in closer to Kaylin, his eyes never wavering. "Use someone else's kid. Mine isn't available."

Benji lifted his chin. "Dad, I can handle it."

The man's nostrils flared. "Can you guarantee my son's protection?"

Nothing was absolute, but Hudson would try. "We will be there with him every step of the way. As soon as the dealer emerges and offers more drugs to Benji, we'll move in."

The teen fished his cell phone out of his pocket. "I'm doing it, Dad." He typed a message.

They waited.

Would the dealer take the bait?

Hudson kept his anticipation under control, though he knew this could be the break they were looking for. The clock on the wall ticked, the only sound in the classroom. He eyed Kaylin. She bit her lip, something he'd already learned was a nervous habit. He knew she was as anxious as he was to find this ring.

A couple minutes later the boy's cell phone dinged.

"What did they say?" Kaylin asked.

"After a few swear words, they agreed." Benji threw his phone down. "What do we do now?"

Hudson gestured toward the door. "You're coming with us to the station. We have paperwork to do and then we have to get you wired." He glanced at his watch. Twelve thirty. They had a few hours to get ready for this exchange. "Please, sir, we need to know if we have your permission. Time is running out."

David poked his finger into Hudson's chest. "Fine, but

if something happens to Benji, I'm holding you person-
ally responsible."

Hudson rubbed his neck, massaging the forming knots.
*No pressure.*

Kaylin's heart pounded in anticipation of the upcom-
ing meet. The thought of putting a boy's life in danger
ate away at her like a mouse gnawing on a box of tissues.
But what choice did they have? They needed to catch this
ring and she would do everything in her power to make
that happen. After all, her father counted on her to get
the job done. This would be one ring gone off the never-
ending list of drug smugglers. Plus, she needed to take
the target off her back.

She scrolled through her texts to pass the time and calm
her pulsating nerves. They had everything in place. Benji
sat in the cruiser's back seat as they parked two blocks
down from the school's lot, hidden by a row of cedar trees.
At the station, Hudson had prepped Benji on what to say
and do, and the boy ran through it again, his knee bounc-
ing nervously. The constable had shared the news of his
nephew's coma and it was clear from his agitated state
that he was concerned. For obvious reasons he wanted
this case solved as fast as possible.

She glanced out the window. She couldn't see them but
she knew other officers were strategically placed around
the school, keeping watch.

Her cell phone vibrated and she swiped to check the
newest text. It was from Diane Smith, her long-time friend
who'd taken her in when she'd needed to get away from
her father. Kaylin pictured the elderly woman rocking
while knitting a scarf for the local mission. She was the
only person Kaylin could count on.

Praying 4 u 2day.

How did the woman do it? She always seemed to know when something of significance was happening in Kaylin's life.

Appreciate it, but not sure if God is here.

Why did Diane always have to bring God into everything? Even after all these years, she still trusted in someone she couldn't see or touch. Not Kaylin. She needed proof of God's existence. She just couldn't believe in an entity who supposedly watched over her. Where had He been when her father had ridiculed her at every turn? When Kaylin had lived on the street? God had been nowhere to be seen or heard.

He's always there. U just have 2 believe.

I can't.

Keep looking up. Luv u.

U 2. XO

Kaylin checked the clock on her phone. 5:52 p.m. She turned to Hudson. "It's time to get into place. You ready, Benji?"

"Ready as I'll ever be."

They piled out of the cruiser and Hudson checked the wire once more. "You're good to go. We'll be around the building, watching and ready to take action. Just get him to offer you the drugs. Then we'll move in and make the arrest."

The boy nodded. His hands shook as he buttoned his shirt closed.

Kaylin squeezed his arm. "You'll be okay. Trust us."

Hudson nudged him forward. "Go ahead. We'll follow and get in position."

Benji shuffled toward the school parking lot.

"This better work," Kaylin said.

"It's in God's hands."

Not him, too. She patted her weapon. "No, it's up to us to keep that boy safe." She couldn't believe in an invisible God. "Let's take our places around the corner before the dealer arrives. Benji is counting on us."

Hudson scowled and gestured for her to take the lead. "After you."

Why had she just been rude to this man? She knew better than that. Talk of God always put her in a foul mood.

*Concentrate. You need to help solve the case to prove to your father you're worthy of this job.* She remembered how Hudson had taken over the previous investigation they worked on together. She would not let that happen again.

They reached the corner of the school and Hudson pulled out his binoculars, focusing them in Benji's direction.

Kaylin crouched behind a massive flowerpot and peeked out.

Still no sign of the dealer. She checked her watch. It was 6:05 p.m. She tapped her finger on the side of her leg. Patience was never her strongest virtue. "He's not coming."

Hudson pointed the binoculars to the left, then right. "Give him time. He's not that—"

Tires screeched around the corner and a dented Chevy Impala pulled into the school parking lot, burning rubber. The foul smell lingered in the air.

Kaylin wrinkled her nose and adjusted her earpiece. "Here we go."

A lanky man stepped out of the car and approached Benji.

"Didn't we just give you some drugs?" His deep voice crackled through Kaylin's ear.

"I sold it all." Benji's broken words revealed his nervousness.

*Calm down, kid. You've got this.*

"That fast? Trying to make employee of the month?"

Benji shoved his hands in his pockets and shrugged. "Do you have the goods or not?" His voice steady.

*Good save.*

Kaylin grabbed Hudson's binoculars. Her fingers grazed his, tingling from the electricity surging through. What was that? They'd had a moment earlier when they bumped into each other and she caught something in his gaze. Admiration? She had sworn off men, so why the sudden interest in him? *Concentrate, Kaylin! You have a job to do.*

She studied the suspect. The man slouched over and reached into his car. His shoulder-length curly hair swung forward, hiding his face. He tucked it behind his ear and passed Benji a package, revealing his tattooed arm. He snatched it back, eyes narrowing. "You get it when you give me money. Your rich father footing the bill?"

"That's none of your business." Benji pulled out a wad of cash.

The lanky man reached for it.

Hudson pulled out his weapon. "That's it. Move in."

Kaylin stood from her position, holding her gun in front of her body.

They rushed around the corner and across the parking lot.

"Stop, police!" Hudson raised his Smith & Wesson. "Turn around and place your hands on the hood."

The drug dealer dropped the package and grabbed Benji. He pulled out a gun and held it to the boy's temple. "Don't come any closer or I swear I'll shoot."

Hudson and Kaylin froze in their tracks.

"Give it up, man." Hudson took a step forward. "You're surrounded."

Officers emerged from their stakeout locations and circled the suspect with their weapons raised.

The lanky man squeezed Benji harder. "Is this boy's life worth the risk?"

"Is yours?" Kaylin hated attitudes like this one. Did he really think he could get away from them? He'd be shot if he fired his weapon.

He pushed the boy aside, raising his hands and gun. "I surrender. It's not me you want anyway. I'm just a small piece of the big pie."

Hudson rushed the man and grabbed the Glock out of his hand, stuffing it into the back of his pants. He spun him around and slammed him against the car's hood. "Who do you work for?" He cuffed him.

"I ain't saying nothing until I call my lawyer."

Hudson's cell phone dinged. He checked his text message, then relayed it to Kaylin. "Finally, a break. We caught the van's driver from this morning."

"Excellent. Maybe he can lead us to whoever is behind all this. Too many small fish in the big pond." Kaylin holstered her weapon.

Hudson shoved the lanky man forward to another officer. "Book him."

"Yes, sir." The constable led the suspect away.

Hudson patted Benji on the back. "Great job, man. You held up under the pressure. The authorities will take what you've done here into consideration. We'll drop you off at the station. Your father is waiting."

Benji's eyes clouded and his gaze shifted to the pavement.

Kaylin picked up on his actions. Obviously, something about his father unnerved him.

She placed a hand on Benji's arm. "You okay?"

His gaze snapped to hers. "I'm fine." His tone was curt.

Did this boy have trouble with his father? She flexed her fingers. *Just because you had father issues doesn't mean everyone does.*

The boy slouched his shoulders and headed to the vehicle.

Clearly there was more to his story.

And Kaylin desperately wanted to know. She couldn't save herself from past heartache, but could she help a troubled teen?

Her cell phone rang and she glanced at the number. *Speaking of fathers.* She gritted her teeth before answering. "What's up?"

"Is that how you greet your father?"

"I'm busy, Dad. We're working on a lead." Did she have to justify everything to him?

His exaggerated sigh passed through the cell phone. "Listen, there's been a development."

"What?"

"I just received a disturbing picture a moment ago. I'm sending it to you now."

Kaylin held her breath. Him, too?

"I'm pulling you off this case."

How could she convince him that she needed to stop the drug smugglers? Even if it meant putting her own life in jeopardy. "No, you're not."

"Look at the picture, Kaylin. You need to be careful."

She pulled the phone down to check it out.

It was a picture of her standing with Benji and Hudson at the school. Her face had an X through it with a caption below it.

Stop this task force or your daughter will die.

* * *

Hudson scratched on his notepad while waiting for the driver of the florist van to be brought into the interrogation room. He wanted to record what went down at the meet. They couldn't miss a beat in this investigation. Kaylin sat across from him, checking her cell phone. She had shared the latest picture with him and the conversation she'd had with her father. It seemed they'd stepped on an anthill and now smugglers were exploding onto the scene, targeting the task force. He was more determined than ever to stop them.

They'd dropped Benji off to his father and even though the teen had seemed reluctant to go, his father had insisted they leave right away. He'd also promised to sue the department if his son had any lasting nightmares over this incident. Didn't seem to matter that Benji had scored a victory with this takedown and would probably get off with just community service. David Rossiter had practically dragged his son down the hall and out the door.

"There's something about Benji's father I don't trust." Kaylin tossed her cell phone onto the table and stood. "Benji didn't seem to want to go with him. Did you get that impression, too?"

"Perhaps an overprotective father?"

She shook her head. "There's more to it. I can sense it."

How could she possibly know, he wondered. "What makes you say that?"

"The way Benji acted around his father. He's almost scared of him."

Hudson ran his hand along the metal table. Its coolness soothed his sweaty fingers. "You think he'll hurt him or something?"

"I know the signs." Her eyes darkened.

Instinctively he knew there was a story behind her sullen expression. "How do you know?"

She stood up and paced the tiny room. "I just do."

Clearly, he wouldn't get more out of her, but he sure wanted to know what she was hiding.

The door opened, and a guard ushered in the van driver, pushing him into the chair. He cuffed his hands to the metal bar fastened to the table. "No more trouble out of you, mister." The guard threw a folder in front of Hudson.

"He giving you problems?" Hudson opened the file and glanced at the particulars. Akio Lee, age twenty-six, resident of Toronto. Two arrests for drug trafficking. One for assault with a deadly weapon. Another for attempted rape. A passport picture of another man also lined the inside of the folder. Martin Belliveau.

"Nothing I can't handle." He rubbed his reddened cheek. "He's all yours, Constable." The guard slammed the door on the way out.

"You taking potshots at the guard, Mr. Lee?" Hudson said.

"Whatever." The man slouched in his chair.

"Seems you have quite the dossier of crimes." Hudson handed the file to Kaylin.

She opened it and read it before dropping it on the table. "Where's your partner, Akio?"

Akio shrugged. "Don't know. We parted ways."

Hudson leaned forward. "Right after you torched the van?"

"I know nothing, man. I'm just a driver for a florist."

Kaylin huffed. "A driver with a list of felonies a mile long."

"That's in the past. I've changed my ways."

"Hardly. Tell us what you were transporting into the

country. Whatever it was you didn't want us to find."
Kaylin sat opposite him.

"Flowers."

Hudson tilted his head. "You can get flowers in Canada. Why were they coming from the US?"

"I don't know. Something about a rare breed of roses." He jiggled the cuffs in front of him, clanging against the bar. "You have nothing on me. Let me go."

Kaylin placed her hands on the table, leaning close to Akio. "Nothing on you? You fired on an officer of the law. Why did you have a picture of me and the police chief?"

"I was only following orders."

Hudson leaned forward. "By whom?"

"Don't know."

Hudson's chest tightened, his unconscious nephew entering his mind. "How could you not know?"

Silence.

"What about the knife behind your driver's seat? What were you going to use that for?" Kaylin massaged her forehead. "And stop lying to us."

"That's only for opening boxes."

Hudson lunged out of his chair. "Tell us the truth. What was in that van?" He paused. "If you cooperate, we'll try to help you."

"Yeah, right. You'll put me behind bars and let me rot. I know what a cop's promise can do."

"You have experience, I take it?" Kaylin fiddled with the strap on her radio. "Look, we don't want you. We want your boss. Cooperate with us and we'll try to get you a plea bargain."

Could they? Hudson wasn't so sure. But they'd let him believe that.

Akio bit his lip.

They had him nervous now. Good.

"He'll kill me," Akio whispered.

It was the second time they'd heard that today. First the boy and now this man. Both were scared of someone. But who?

Kaylin's eyes softened. "We can protect you, Mr. Lee. Tell us what you know."

"My partner did all the dealing with the boss man. I was only supposed to drive the van to and from the States."

Hudson sat back down and picked up his pen. "What's your partner's name?"

"Blaine Ridley."

He checked the file. "Says here it's Martin Belliveau." He shoved the passport picture in front of Akio. "This him?"

"Nope. He obviously used a fake passport."

How did he get across the border, then? Then he remembered Kaylin mentioning he wore a hoodie, hiding his face from her.

Hudson wrote down the name. "Can you give us a description of him? Any distinguishable features?"

"About six feet. Bushy hair, beard. Zigzag scar under his right eye. Said he got it in a bar fight."

Not a lot to go on, but Hudson would get a sketch made. "What was the plan for your shipment?"

"We would cross at the Windsor border and pick up the flower order in Detroit, then make our way back with all the correct papers."

"If you only had flowers, why would we think anything of it? Why pull a gun?" Kaylin scooted her chair closer to the driver, obviously wanting to intimidate him.

He shrugged. His knee bounced as if he was ready to bolt if he could.

"Who are you scared of?" Hudson guessed the man wasn't telling them everything. His nervousness proved it.

Akio chewed on his fingernails. "He promised he'd kill us if we ever told anyone about him."

"Do you know who he is?" Kaylin rubbed the back of her neck.

"We only know him as—"

A rumble shook the building.

The lights snapped off, leaving them in pitch darkness.

# FOUR

Kaylin flicked on her flashlight as adrenaline coursed through her body. Was this a simple power outage or something more sinister? Her mind raced to the latter. It was too much of a coincidence after everything else that had happened today. Had they found her? Her father's warning echoed in her mind. She rested her right hand on her holstered weapon. No way would she be caught unaware.

Across from her, Akio's eyes widened. "What's going on?"

A crash sounded down the hall, followed by screams.

"He's found me." Akio's whimper didn't fit with the image of the arrogant van driver he'd portrayed earlier.

Hudson bolted out of his chair, unleashing his gun. "I'll check it out. Stay here with him." He rushed out of the room.

Kaylin set the flashlight on the table. "Who do you think has found you? What are you involved in?"

Akio exhaled. "I needed the job, man."

"What exactly is your job? Drug running across the border? Targeting people?"

His eyes flashed in the beam of light. "No."

"Why did you torch the van?"

The man's knee bounced. His obvious nervous tic. "Blaine told me the boss man would get angry if the shipment fell into the police's hands. Plus, we made sure you saw the pictures as he said we needed to scare you so your father would back off. The boss ordered it. I do what I'm told. Learned that from living in the hood."

Kaylin certainly related to living among danger. She'd faced it in her short time with the homeless as they defended their territory. Fights broke out frequently and she had done her best to steer clear of them. She shuddered. Thank God for Diane, who'd saved her from that life. *Did I just thank God?* She wasn't thinking straight. It was all Diane. God had nothing to do with it. She rubbed her brow and concentrated on the situation in front of her. Enough about her past. She needed to figure out this case quickly and bring down this ring.

Before they got to her or her father.

"Tell me about your boss man. Do you know his name?"

He massaged his neck. "Blaine only referred to him as Valentino."

"Have you met him?" She wrote the name down.

"No, not many have. All I know is he has men everywhere." He leaned forward, eyes narrowing. "You better watch your back. They're close and watching."

"How do you know that?" How far did this drug ringleader's tentacles reach? How many people were involved? The thought of anyone hurting her family or friends sent a jolt of anger through her veins. She had to stop them.

"Blaine is always nervous and said one of them confronted him when he stole money. They roughed him up and said never to cheat Valentino again. That was when he knew they were watching. He's been paranoid ever since."

"Where's Blaine now?"

Akio shrugged. "Don't know. He ran in one direction and told me to go in the other. That we couldn't be seen together."

"Can you get in touch with him? He's our only hope to finding out more about Valentino and what they're smuggling."

"I can give you the address where I picked him up for this run."

Kaylin slid her notepad and pen across the table. "Write it down."

Akio scribbled on the paper. "I've cooperated, so can you give me a deal?"

"That will be for Constable Steeves to decide. This is his case."

"What do you—"

The door opened and Hudson entered. "We have to leave. Now." He unlocked Akio's cuffs and pulled him up.

Kaylin grabbed her flashlight and stood. "What's going on?"

"Bomb threat. They're clearing the building."

"Where do we go?" Kaylin's head throbbed, but she ignored it.

"To the nearest OPP station. We're transporting all our prisoners there. We can finish our interrogations after we're secured. We still have to question our drug dealer suspect."

Akio wiggled in Hudson's vise grip. "How about you give me a deal?"

"You need to provide us with more intel before that can happen," Hudson said.

"But I gave her lots of info."

Hudson raised his brow. "Until I'm satisfied, you'll stay with us."

"But they're watching. They probably called in this threat and caused the power outage." He paused. "They know I'm here."

"Who?" Hudson said.

"Like I told Officer Poirier, I only know him as Valentino. Blaine told me they're never far away. You have to let me go, man. I'm not safe with her." He pointed toward Kaylin.

She dismissed the quiver of fear running down her neck and tucked her notepad into her vest pocket. She understood the man's concerns. It seemed this ring stretched far and wide. "You're the safest you can be. We'll protect you. Cooperate with us."

"I am! I told you everything."

"Have you?" She raised a brow.

He cursed and looked at his feet. "Yes."

Kaylin knew that expression. Either he was too scared to say anything or he was holding back because he was more involved than he let on.

And she intended to find out which.

Hudson pushed him toward the door. "We need to clear the building. We've already wasted valuable time."

Kaylin followed the pair out of the room and down the darkened hall.

An officer ushered their other drug dealer suspect, the lanky man from the high school parking lot, out the front door.

The evening breeze kissed Kaylin's cheek and she welcomed the fresh night air after a humid day. Officers rushed by, vacating the building, as two shots pierced the night, echoing around them.

Kaylin drew in a sharp breath.

Beside her, Akio fell to the pavement, along with the drug dealer.

Both lay in a pool of blood.

Hudson crouched and whipped out his 9 mm, pointing it in the direction of the shots. They were out in the open and easy targets. A suspicion raced through his mind. Someone must've called in a fake bomb threat to get them out of the building so they could take out both suspects.

Who were these people and how closely were they being watched?

Akio lay motionless. Taken out by a shot to the forehead. Assassin style. The man had probably died instantly.

Hudson placed himself in front of Kaylin. He needed to protect her from the hidden enemy. He waited for more shots.

But none came.

The shooter had hit the assigned targets. And in so doing, he had killed Hudson's first big break in this case.

Heat flushed through his body as he pictured Matthew on his hospital bed. Still. Silent. The life sucked out of him. Hudson's only lead had faded like a weathered photograph while his nephew's assailant goes free. *I can't fail him, Lord.*

The drug dealer they'd arrested in the school parking lot moaned.

Hudson checked the man's pulse. It was weak. They had to get him to the hospital immediately.

He grimaced and holstered his gun. He had a job to do. "We're clear. Seems the shooter only wanted these two. Our drug dealer is still alive." He pulled out his cell phone and called for EMS. He motioned to another officer. "Put pressure on his wound until the paramedics get here. We need this guy alive. He has valuable information in our case."

The constable obeyed and placed his gloved hands on the lanky man's chest.

Kaylin put her gun away. "How did these people know we had both men?"

"I don't know."

"Akio did say he was being watched. Could it be the same sniper who took shots at us at the border?"

"Probably. Who else would it be?" It was the only active case Hudson was working on at the moment. Was he getting closer?

Hudson eyed the dead witness. What information died with Akio? He knew the driver had held back information, but what? "What did Mr. Lee tell you after I left the room?"

"Gave me the name Valentino as the head of the ring. Also said he didn't know much, but he gave me an address for Blaine Ridley."

He glanced at his watch. 8:30 p.m. "Want to check it out?"

Distant sirens sounded.

"It's getting late and we haven't eaten since lunch."

"What? You going to turn into a pumpkin?"

She scowled, taking a wide-legged stance. "Fine, boss. We'll do as you wish."

*Ouch.* What gave him the right to be rude? He rubbed his temples as a migraine hovered in the background. Stress held him in its grip. He obviously hadn't learned from their past working relationship. "Sorry. Didn't mean to be insensitive."

An ambulance and OPP officers pulled in front of them. Paramedics scrambled out of their vehicle and relieved the officer holding pressure on the suspect. "We'll take it from here."

"Jacobs, follow them to the hospital," Hudson said to one of the constables. "I want a report on his condition later. We still need to question him."

The officer nodded and raced to his vehicle.

"He won't be in any condition for your questions, sir. At least until after surgery," the paramedic said as he hooked the suspect up to a portable IV and sped him away without waiting for further comments.

The coroner arrived moments later to take Akio's body to the morgue.

Hudson shook his head. What a waste. This young van driver was struck down in his prime. Whatever future he'd had had evaporated. *Lord, be with his family as they go through their loss.* Not that he knew if he even had one, but someone out there must have loved this poor guy.

"Do you want to quit for the night and start fresh tomorrow morning?" He gestured for more officers to come forward. "These constables will secure the scene and Forensics will soon be here to check for evidence."

"No way." She pulled a granola bar from her pocket and held it up. "My go-to nourishment on the job." She pursed her lips before opening the bar and taking a bite.

Her expression told him he'd annoyed her. He seemed to have a habit of doing that.

He motioned her toward his cruiser and followed her, admiring her from a distance, despite his warnings to himself to keep his eyes averted. Even her uniform couldn't hide her exquisite features. He shook his head. No, he couldn't get wrapped up in past thoughts of this woman. He'd sworn off women since Rebecca. No way would he fall that hard again.

He promised his heart he wouldn't. But sometimes the head and heart didn't agree.

He opened the passenger-side door for her.

She ignored his gallantry and didn't look at him when she climbed into the vehicle, her disdain evident. Could he get through the walls she'd obviously built around her?

He slipped into the driver's seat and started the car. "What address did Akio give you?"

She mumbled it off between bites.

He punched it into his vehicle's GPS and turned right out of the parking lot, heading in the direction of Blaine's home. "How did you get into the CBSA?" It was time to lighten the tension between them. After all, her lousy mood was his fault.

"I saw an ad and it interested me, so I enrolled. They accepted my application and that was that. I love what I do. Keeping the border safe is my passion," she replied.

Her demeanor changed with talk of the CBSA. The lines on her face turned upward from scowls to smiles.

"Your father must be proud," he said.

She heaved a sigh. "I doubt it."

"Why would you say that?"

"We rarely speak."

He turned left onto a side street. "I've seen you together before. You seem so close."

"Don't believe everything you see."

There was a story there. Would she trust him enough to share it? "Well, you're good at what you do," he said. "You proved that to me on our last case when we wired you to get a confession out of your ex for drug trafficking. What was his name again?"

She looked away but not before he caught her frown. How quickly her mood changed again.

"Jake Shepherd, and he's locked up."

"How did you two meet?" There was more behind those sad eyes than she would probably admit, he knew, but he'd try to get it out of her.

She shifted in her seat. "It was after high school, at a church function."

He raised a brow. Maybe she did have a background with the gospel. "So you believe in God?"

"I don't. I went to appease a friend." She fumbled with her shirt button as if trying to occupy her mind with something other than her past.

Another story for another time.

"What happened with Jake?" He turned the police radio down slightly, so he could hear her every word.

She gave up on the button and peered out the window but waited before continuing in a soft voice. "We met, fell in love, got engaged, and then I realized he was doing drugs. But it was after—"

She stopped. Her silence betrayed her tangled emotions.

But he had to know. "After what?" He turned down another street, taking them closer to Blaine's address.

Her eyes glared at him like a cobra ready to strike. "Nothing."

"Didn't he threaten you when you helped convict him?" He couldn't let it go.

She rubbed her arms as if protecting herself from her ex's advances. "He said he'd get even with me when he got out." Her voice broke.

"Good thing he's in jail." *Lord, protect her and help her move past this.*

Kaylin bit her lip.

Her nervous habit. It was cute. *Where did that thought come from?*

"His lawyer is appealing his sentence." Her face turned ashen as she stared at the road ahead.

She was scared, he realized. This man had gotten to her even from behind bars. "Have you heard from him since he was incarcerated?"

"Numerous times. Letters I haven't opened."

"Maybe you should. If they're threats, they could keep him behind bars."

"I don't want to have anything to do with that man." She clamped her mouth shut.

That was his cue to stop talking about her ex. Instead,

he pulled in front of the address given to them. "We're here."

Graffiti filled the front of the dilapidated apartment building with boarded-up windows. Weeds poked out of cracks in the concrete and chunks of brick lay around the yard.

"Wow. How can anyone live here?" Kaylin opened her door. "Looks like the building is ready to be condemned."

"Let's be careful. This may be a setup."

She shook her head. "No, Akio seemed to want to help. I don't think he fed me incorrect information."

"Only one way to find out. Let's go."

She walked up the uneven sidewalk ahead of him, side-stepping the bulging concrete.

The front door hung at an angle, broken at the hinges.

Young boys played basketball in the lot next to the building under lights. Shouldn't they be home now with their parents? This rough neighborhood could easily cause problems for these boys. "When will kids learn to get off the street at night? Especially here."

"I wonder if their parents know where they are."

Hudson eased open the broken door. "What apartment?"

"Second floor. Number two fourteen."

Their footsteps creaked on the old stairs. No keeping their arrival quiet. Hudson walked with his hand ready on his weapon. He wasn't taking any chances. He opened the door to the second level and the overwhelming scent of marijuana filled the air.

Hudson crinkled his nose. "Great. This building has got to be a grow-op."

"No wonder it appears abandoned."

The smell increased the closer they got to their destination.

Hudson pointed. "Here's two fourteen."

The door stood ajar, its lock broken.

Hudson unholstered his weapon and eased the door open.

"Looks like someone beat us here."

Kaylin whisked out her weapon and followed Hudson into the ransacked apartment. Tables were overturned, couch and chairs ripped to shreds, and marijuana plants strewn about the one-bedroom apartment. A skunky odor filled the small area and Kaylin covered her nose and mouth with her hand. The cannabis reeked.

Hudson raised his gun and swept the room. "Police. Anyone here?" He turned back. "Check the bedroom."

She entered the tiny room ready to take action. It, too, was trashed. Mattress torn apart, dresser drawers open with the contents thrown all over, but no sign of Blaine.

"Clear." She moved back into the living room. "The place is empty. Sure looks like someone was bent on finding something."

"Agreed. I wonder what Blaine had that they so desperately wanted."

She holstered her weapon. "And who are they? Can this all be related to the drug smuggling ring or something else?"

"Good questions." He pulled out his cell phone. "I'll call it in. Maybe we can get prints from this mess."

Would they? Considering the way their day had gone so far, she doubted it.

A wave of dizziness plagued her and she teetered. She grabbed the back of the couch to steady herself. The day had taken its toll on her. She needed to get home, eat a real meal and climb into a hot bath to soothe her achy body.

No. She would not let Hudson see her as weak. She'd

struggled too hard to get to where she was, given all the criticism from her male coworkers. She'd prove them wrong, especially her father. One way to do that was to solve this case. Even if it meant putting her own life at risk. And working with another male. At least this one wasn't hard on the eyes, and he seemed kinder this time around.

*Did I just think that?* She blinked. No way would she be caught in the same situation as she was with Jake. No, she didn't trust men. Not after her broken engagement.

But it was hard not to notice the handsome man beside her, with his army-cut hairstyle and muscular arms. He piqued her interest.

But she had to stop thinking about him.

Besides, he believed in God. Something they could never agree on.

She glanced at her watch. "Are we done after the forensic unit arrives?"

He clenched his jaw. "I need to keep going. Find these people." His face twisted, the pain evident.

She placed a hand on his arm. "I'm sorry about your nephew, but you won't help him by overtaxing yourself. Believe me, I want to catch these people, too, but it's been a long day and you need rest. We both do."

His shoulders squared as if preparing for battle.

His love for his nephew drove him. She understood that, but she wouldn't let him wear himself out. Matthew needed him alert. "You know I'm right. Don't fight me on this."

He let out a forced breath and his muscles relaxed. "Fine. We'll call it a night." He stuffed his phone back into his pocket. "Forensics should be here within ten minutes."

"Good." She spotted a drug kit on the coffee table. "Looks like Blaine here dabbles in his business. I wonder if it's doda."

"The unit will test it to find out. Wouldn't surprise me if it was doda, since it appears he's involved."

"How do you know that?"

Hudson stared at the mess in the living room. "He ran, didn't he? I suspect he knew more than Akio and that's why he's on the run."

"We need to have someone stake out this place in case he returns."

"I'll clear that with my sergeant." Once again, he pulled out his phone to make the call.

The front door squeaked open. "You two aren't messing up the crime scene, are you?" Bianca walked in with the Ident team. They set their kit on the floor and pulled out fingerprint powder.

Kaylin held her hands in front of her, palms out. "We haven't touched a thing. I promise."

Hudson clicked off his call. "Hey, Bianca. Good to see you again." He gestured around the apartment. "Think you guys will be able to get some prints off this mess?"

"We'll do our best." She put on her gloves.

"You find out anything from the van?"

"The team hasn't had much time for the tests yet, but nothing so far. Doesn't look hopeful. Whatever was in the van was completely destroyed."

Hudson frowned. "We need to see if there's any connection to the doda smuggling ring."

"You'll be the first to know." She opened her notebook. "For now, leave us so they can do their job."

"We're outta here." Hudson motioned Kaylin toward the door. "Time to get you a protective detail at your address."

She scoffed. "No way. I know how to protect myself."

"And your police chief father would have my head if I let something happen to you. Don't argue."

She realized it was his turn to be forceful. So she just shook her head and followed him out of the apartment.

An hour later, with an officer positioned in front of her building, Kaylin let the lavender-scented candle permeate the air in her living room. She slouched back into the couch, allowing her achy muscles to relax. Exactly what she needed after a long day.

Her black-and-white cat hopped onto the coffee table. She stuck her paw into Kaylin's ice water and licked it.

Kaylin giggled. "Sassme, why do you do that?"

The cat meowed.

Kaylin kissed the feline's forehead before it jumped down and trotted out of the room.

Her cell phone rang, jarring her out of a relaxed state. Who could be calling at eleven thirty? She reached for her phone and when she saw an unknown caller, she hit the decline button. She didn't want to talk to anyone tonight.

The cell phone rang again.

Same unknown caller.

Someone was persistent. She picked up. "Poirier here."

Silence. Heavy breathing.

"Hello? Who's there?"

"I'm watching you."

Kaylin sat up straight. "Who's this?"

"You're mine."

*Click.*

Goose bumps spiked the hair on her arms.

So much for a relaxing evening. There was no way she'd be able to sleep tonight.

# FIVE

Hudson arrived early the next morning at the police station to research the Saskatchewan doda bust and gather all the information he could. The more he knew the better. Constable Larry Jacobs had called after Hudson dropped Kaylin off last night and told him the drug dealer had been rushed into surgery as soon as they arrived at the hospital. The man had made it out alive but he was critical. Hudson would question him today.

The bomb squad had cleared their station, proving Hudson's theory that the fake threat was only a ruse to get them to exit the building and expose the driver and the dealer to assassins. Hudson left the description of Blaine Ridley with Bianca. She would arrange for a rough sketch so they could circulate it.

He rubbed his temples, trying to ward off another pending migraine. His lack of sleep had triggered an aura earlier and he knew what was coming. He grabbed his prescription meds and popped one in his mouth. His day required a clear mind and he wouldn't be able to function with a throbbing head.

His cell phone rang. He swiped the screen and saw an incoming call from his best friend, Layke Jackson in Calgary. "Hey, bud. Isn't it early there?" He hit the search icon on his computer and waited as the cursor circled.

The two had met at the local mission when they were fifteen and hit it off right away. Layke had been living on the streets for a short period of time. They'd stayed in touch over the years and even gone to college to become officers together.

"Just finishing the night shift. How's your case going?"

"Slow. Had a lead yesterday, but a shooter took him out. Another suspect is fighting for his life in the hospital."

"Tough break. Who are you working with?"

"Kaylin Poirier from the CBSA."

Layke whistled. "Oooo...her again, huh?"

"I hear the tone in your voice. Forget it. I've sworn off women, remember?" A link to the Saskatchewan drug bust appeared on his screen. He clicked on it and took a sip of coffee.

Layke clucked his tongue. "You need to get over Rebecca. Not all women are cheaters like her. Besides, it's been almost a year. Time to move on."

Hudson winced. He knew his friend was right, but Rebecca's cheating ways had done a number on him. *Lord, help me get over her and trust in You.* "Speaking of moving on, let's talk about something else. You on a case right now?"

"I think I'll be working soon on one concerning a child trafficking ring. We've caught wind of it happening here in Alberta as well as at the Yukon border."

"Those poor kids. I hate hearing stuff like that. They're so young when they're ripped from their families."

"I know. They're being used in sweatshops across the country."

"I hope you get on the team."

"Me, too. Means I'll also be working with the CBSA."

Kaylin came through the door carrying a large coffee and rubbing her eyes. She waved and smiled when she spied him and headed in his direction, her ponytail swaying as she walked.

She was beautiful. He couldn't help but notice. He

raked his fingers through his stubbled hair and admonished himself. *Concentrate.*

"They're a good agency. Sworn to protect the borders." He finished his coffee and threw out the paper cup. "Listen, I gotta run. Kaylin is here and we're headed to the hospital to question a suspect."

"Stay safe, buddy. Chat later."

"You got it."

They clicked off the call as Kaylin reached his desk.

"Morning," she said through a yawn.

"You not sleep last night?" He noticed the dark patches under her eyes.

"Unfortunately not. Had a disturbing call before bed. Put me on edge."

Hudson sat straight, his protective senses on alert. "What kind of call?"

She pulled up a chair beside him. "Someone said they were watching me." She twirled the end of her ponytail.

He leaned back and blew out a breath. "The smugglers?"

She blinked rapidly before taking another sip. "Who else could it be?" She rubbed her palm on the front of her pants, over and over.

This caller had gotten to her more than she was willing to admit. "Well, someone out there is after you." He reached for his phone. "We need to call your father. Give him an update."

She placed her hand on top of the receiver, brushing his fingers.

A jolt raced through his arm from her simple touch. What was that?

She snapped her hand back and he looked up at her.

Her eyes looked focused and determined when she spoke. "Please don't. He threatened to take me off the case before and I need to finish this. I'm fine. I'll call my phone carrier and get a new number."

So she was still the stubborn officer he remembered from the last time they worked together. "Don't you think it's better to be safe than sorry?"

She glared at him. "I can take care of myself, Hudson."

He couldn't win. All he wanted was to keep her safe. "Not saying you can't, but this seems like a threat to me."

She eyed the report on his screen. "That the latest seizure?"

Nothing like changing the subject. "Yes, they seized nearly a thousand grams of doda at the Saskatchewan border."

"Any arrests?"

"They captured a thirty-five-year-old man and charged him under the Controlled Drugs and Substances Act." He scrolled through the report. "However, a lawyer got him off on a technicality. Seems the arresting officer didn't follow the correct protocol."

"Sounds like a good lawyer."

"Yes, one linked to the dark web."

Kaylin leaned in closer to the screen. "What?"

Her vanilla scent tickled his sinuses. He breathed in deeper, getting lost in the fragrance. Was that her shampoo?

*Focus, Hudson.* "Yes, we've been watching this lawyer on other cases. Seems he has a presence on the dark web and offers his services to those needing to get off drug charges. He works across Canada and has made quite a name for himself."

"Do you think he's linked to our case somehow?"

"Nothing would surprise me."

"Isn't doda a powdered opiate?" Kaylin finished her coffee and threw the cup in the garbage.

Hudson pointed to the screen. "Yep. It's made from crushed poppy seeds, similar to the stash we confiscated from Benji."

He closed the report. "Jacobs called and said the surgery went well on our suspect. Looks like he'll pull through."

"Do we know his name yet?"

"He didn't have any identification on him when we picked him up and he was tight-lipped. We took his prints and are running them against our records in CPIC. We should hear soon."

Hudson and his team used the Canadian Police Information Centre's computerized system to track down criminals and help identify them. He clicked on the application to boot it up. "Actually, let's see if we have a hit yet."

He typed a few keys and once again his cursor circled while they waited.

He peered over his screen and stole a glimpse at Kaylin. Much as he told himself to keep it strictly professional, he had to admit she intrigued him. What was her story? How could he find out without intruding on her personal space? He recalled their previous case hadn't gone well when Hudson had tried to take over. But he'd learned a lot about himself during their investigation. Now that he wanted to know more about Kaylin, he vowed to do better this time around.

"Did you get a chance to talk to your dad last night?"

Her body tensed. "I don't want to talk about him."

"Why not?"

She glared at him. "Let's just say that's uncharted territory and I've blocked him from my life."

How could she not want her own father around? He longed for his, but Ron Steeves had been ripped from his family when Hudson was only a boy. He closed his eyes and pictured the pool of blood.

So much blood.

A tremor crept in and he blinked to rid himself of the dreadful image. It was a day he wished he could change. But nothing could amend history or take away the suffering. "Sorry to hear that. I wish I still had a dad."

"Not one like mine, you don't." She tapped her thumb on his desk.

*Interesting.*

"And you said your brother and mother are both passed. So you don't have any other family?"

"Just a woman who took me in after I lost all hope. Her name is Diane Smith, and she's like you."

"What do you mean?"

"A Christian."

He picked up on the tone of her voice. "Why are you so negative about Christians?"

"I can't stand the hypocrisy. My father was one person in church and another in our home. All talk but no action. Always judging."

"We're not all the same."

Granted, a lot were exactly as she described. However, most weren't. He hated that she'd pegged them all with the same attitude.

Her eyes brightened. "You're right. Diane is different. She took me in for a period of time and treated me like I was her own daughter. I'll never forget that."

"I'm glad you had someone like her."

She looked away. "Me, too," she whispered.

A ding on his computer jolted him from their conversation. He leaned closer. "Looks like we got a hit." He scrolled through the entry. "Our suspect is Percy Brown."

He clicked the link to pull up the record. "It appears

Mr. Brown has been in and out of jail. Armed robbery, numerous drug trafficking busts and domestic violence."

"Regular nice guy."

"He was paroled six months ago. Well, he certainly didn't learn his lesson, did he?" He stood and grabbed his weapon. "How about we pay Mr. Brown a visit in the hospital?"

"Sounds good to me."

He prayed they'd find out information to bring them closer to busting the ring.

Before more drugs infiltrated the streets and more teens ended up like Matthew.

Kaylin rushed behind Hudson down the corridor of Windsor Regional Hospital. She hated hospitals. They brought nothing but sorrow.

However, this visit was a welcome interruption to their otherwise dreary conversation. No way did Kaylin want to talk about Marshall Poirier to anyone. Her father was a distant thought in her memory bank. She could never forgive the heartache he'd caused. She hated that she had to work with him on this task force. She needed for it to be over so she could go on with her life.

On the drive to the hospital, she placed a call to her cell phone provider and requested a new number and that it be unlisted. She texted it to her father, gave it to Hudson and her boss, plus her closest friends. No one else would have it until this case was over. She wasn't taking any more chances.

They reached Percy Brown's room and the officer on duty stood from his stationed position. "Constable Steeves. Good to see you."

"How is he, Jacobs?"

"The doctor reported this morning that he was stabilized. He's awake, but be careful questioning him. He's frail."

"How long are you on duty?" Hudson said.

"Another three hours. Sergeant wants someone at his door twenty-four/seven."

"Understood, since he was almost taken out yesterday. We need him alive." Hudson paused and pointed toward her. "This is CBSA officer Kaylin Poirier."

"The chief's daughter." Jacobs nodded. "Nice to meet you."

"Has the victim talked at all?" she asked.

"He's been silent, but maybe you guys will get something out of him."

Hudson motioned toward the door. "Let's go see what Mr. Brown can tell us."

Kaylin moved into the darkened room. The heart monitor's beeping intruded on the quietness. Percy Brown lay in his narrow hospital bed. His shallow breathing could barely be heard over the machines. His curly hair was now matted to his head like a bird's nest, while a five o'clock shadow had taken over his chin. He moaned and turned his head back and forth.

Hudson stepped to the side of the bed. "Mr. Brown, are you awake?" He turned on the overhead light.

Percy blinked his eyes open and squinted from the sudden brightness. He scowled when he saw Hudson. "What do you want?"

Kaylin stepped forward. "Mr. Brown, how long have you been dealing drugs?"

"Right to business, I see." He looked out the window. "Only this one time."

He was lying. Why couldn't suspects just tell the truth when they were caught?

Hudson eyed her, raising a brow, and then turned to

Percy. "We don't believe you. How many kids did you sell to?"

"That snot-nosed kid squeal on me?"

"You were caught in the act," Hudson said. "How can you deny it?"

Percy fidgeted with his IV. "I ain't sayin' nothing more. I know my rights."

Kaylin rubbed her temples. She hated it when suspects pulled this card. "Don't you get you were targeted by a sniper? Someone wants you out of the picture."

"Tell us what you know and we'll protect you." Hudson pulled out his notebook.

Percy cringed. "You can't keep me safe. Not from these people."

"What people?" Kaylin grabbed a chair and positioned it beside the bed. "Who are you working for?"

He bit his lip. "They'll go after my family, man. They don't play around."

"We'll make sure they're okay." At least Kaylin hoped so. "Tell us what you know."

"I don't deal with the head honcho. Only his right-hand man, Blaine."

Him again. They needed to find Blaine Ridley and fast.

Hudson moved closer. "How do you contact him?"

"By text. I tell him what I need and he plans the meet."

"So you've never seen him?" Kaylin found that hard to believe.

"Only once, when he didn't have a thug to deliver my goods."

"Can you describe him?" Hudson asked, then when Percy nodded, he said, "We'll get a forensic artist down here to make a composite." Maybe it would be more accurate than the one they're currently working on.

Kaylin hoped they were finally getting somewhere. "What type of drugs do you deal?"

"Anything I can get my hands on, but right now what seems to be popular is the new doda."

"What's new about it?" Kaylin concentrated on the suspect. Could they trust what he told them?

"Not sure. Blaine just said it was more powerful and would give an added kick to my users. More bang for their buck. Who was I to argue?"

"You try it?"

Percy pushed the morphine button. "Nope. Just sell the stuff."

Figured. Another hot shot who liked to get kids high and line his own pockets. Pictures of her brother, Todd, high and useless, popped into her mind. Whenever he used he became lethargic and passed out on the couch, no good to anyone. The last image she remembered of Todd was the needle poking out from his motionless arm. He'd taken too much and it had cost him his life. Kaylin had vowed to fight drugs. Keeping them outside of Canada was her goal at the CBSA and right now they were losing the battle.

They had to get this drug ring off the streets. Before it cost more kids their lives.

But would it mean she wouldn't see Hudson any longer? She was getting used to having him around. Already. His charm was whittling down the wall she'd built. He—

*Pay attention to this case and stop fantasizing.*

Duly chastised by her inner self, she stood and walked to the window, putting distance between herself and Hudson. "Did Blaine ever mention who his boss was?"

"He only referred to him as Valentino, but I never dealt with him."

Kaylin glanced at Hudson.

He raised a brow.

That was the second time they'd heard that name. First by Akio and now Percy.

Hudson sat in Kaylin's chair. "Can you get in touch with him? Set up a meet?"

"With Valentino? Hardly. He never makes appearances. I only deal with Blaine."

Hudson rubbed his head. "Okay, then set up a meet with Blaine. We catch him, we catch Valentino."

"I need my phone. You guys confiscated it."

Hudson handed him his. "Use mine."

"No can do. He knows my number. He'll suspect a trap."

"We'll get it and bring it over later." Hudson stood. "What else—"

"Time's up, people." A nurse sauntered in with a tray of meds. "Mr. Brown needs his medication. Everyone, out."

Kaylin and Hudson left the room.

Jacobs met them in the corridor. "Nurse kick you out?"

"Yup." Hudson closed his notebook and shoved it in his pocket. "We have to get his phone from the station."

Kaylin nodded. "It's the only lead we have. Sounds like we need to get to the top. Both of our suspects named Valentino."

"Agreed," Hudson said.

Minutes later the nurse emerged from the room. "He's sleeping now. You'll have to come back later." She walked down the hall and disappeared.

Hudson shrugged. "So much for him giving us details for a composite."

"Maybe we can come back this afternoon." Kaylin hoped the man would be more alert then. A more detailed sketch of someone within the ring would definitely help.

Another nurse came around the corner with a cart filled

with meds. "Morning, Officers. I need to give Mr. Brown his meds."

Hudson tipped his head to the side. "What do you mean? Another nurse just gave them to him."

Her eyes widened. "What? I'm the nurse on duty who administers the meds."

Hudson, Kaylin and Jacobs rushed into Percy's room.

The man's body shook with seizures and then lay still.

"No!" Hudson ran to his side. "Jacobs, follow where that other woman went. Catch her."

Jacobs ran out of the room, gun in hand.

The nurse rang the call bell. She felt for a pulse and immediately began compressions. "Get back!"

Her coworker appeared. "What happened?"

"Code Blue. Stat. Call for a crash cart." The first nurse stopped her compressions and grabbed a breathing tube. "All of you, out. Now! Let us do our job."

Hudson and Kaylin stood outside the door as a team scrambled in with a crash cart.

A jolt from the defibrillator sounded.

Seconds ticked by.

Another jolt.

A flat beep echoed into the corridor.

They'd lost their only witness.

# SIX

Hudson paced to rid himself of the frustration seeping through his body. How could this have happened right before them? Another witness gone. They'd lost their only lead and all they had was one name.

Valentino.

They would run it against any known felons in their database, but it was unlikely they would find anyone without a full name. He yanked out his phone and called his boss.

"Miller here." His gruff voice boomed in Hudson's ear.

Great, he wasn't in a good mood. After Hudson broke the news, Sergeant Peter Miller would be even grumpier.

"Sarge, it's Hudson. Hate to tell you this, but we lost Percy Brown. Someone posing as a nurse just took him out."

Miller cursed. "How could you let that happen, Steeves?"

Hudson winced. He couldn't win. He'd made a mistake on a previous case and now this. Miller would never let him hear the end of it. He'd paid for his past blunder, and this one wasn't his fault. Who knew the nurse would turn out to be a killer? Her sweet smiling face had fooled all of them. "She wore a uniform and slipped by us. Jacobs is trying to track her down right now."

"Did Brown give you any details before he died?"

"Just that Blaine Ridley is Valentino's right-hand man. Can you run Valentino's and Ridley's names through our database and see if anything pops up?"

"Got it. Steeves, catch this killer so we can bring

down the ring, or I'll put you on desk duty. You hear?"
He clicked off.

Hudson loosened the button on his gray uniform shirt
and pulled at his Kevlar vest. Now he had another reason
to solve this case.

Kaylin grabbed his arm. "You okay?" She left her hand
there.

He felt at home with her touch. Was he crazy? He
needed to concentrate, but she made it hard. "Nothing I
can't handle." At least he hoped so.

"Your boss giving you a hard time over this loss?"

"Yup. Just another mistake to add to my list."

She scrunched her nose. "Another? Have there been
many?"

Not her, too. He stayed silent.

"What happened?" she prompted.

"Let's just say I lost a witness and it was my fault." A
memory he wanted to erase but couldn't.

"How?"

His shoulders drooped. "I waited too long to act and
he drowned."

"When was this?"

"Two years ago. A suspect pushed his hostage into
the water and took off. I froze." He had just gotten a big
lead on the case he'd been investigating and everything
had spiraled from there. He'd been working ever since to
right his wrong.

Her brows furrowed. "You can't swim?"

"I can, but water has always scared me since I was a
boy. When I realized the hostage couldn't swim, I jumped
in, but it was too late. We couldn't resuscitate him." He
studied his shoes. "It's a day I'll never forget and neither
will my boss. Made me go for therapy to get over it."

The coroner arrived and wheeled Percy's body by them

and down the corridor. A forensic pathologist would perform an autopsy to find out what killed him.

"And now you lost this suspect."

He followed Kaylin's gaze to the dead body. "That pretty much sums it up. He's threatened to put me on desk duty if I don't solve this case."

"Accidents happen. He can't hold that over you forever."

"You don't know Sergeant Miller. He's a bully." He toyed with his holster belt, fiddling with the buckle. Would she blame him like everyone else did? He couldn't bear the thought of her disappointment.

She nodded. "Oh, there are a few of those in my department."

"I guess they're everywhere." He studied her face and when he saw no judgment there, he breathed a sigh of relief.

Jacobs and another man walked around the corner, interrupting their conversation. "She's gone. Disappeared. Don't know how. Security checked all entrances."

"She was dressed as a nurse. Probably walked right by everyone." Hudson stuck out his hand to the stranger. "Constable Hudson Steeves."

The burly man shook Hudson's hand with a firm grip. "Paul Dawson. Head of Security at Windsor Regional."

He gestured toward Kaylin. "This is Kaylin Poirier of the CBSA. She's working with us on this case. Do we know how this woman could pose as a nurse so easily?"

"My guess is she had a fake identification card and got past everyone that way. Or—"

"—she really was a nurse," Kaylin said. "One bought by the smuggling ring."

Hudson nodded. "Can we check your security footage? Maybe we'll find something."

"Yes, come with me. Our office is on this floor."

They followed Paul around the corner and into a security area. Guards sat behind a collage of screens. Individuals coming and going passed by the cameras.

"Surely we caught her on tape." Hudson brightened and glanced at his watch. "Take us to Mr. Brown's hall at about ten o-five. That was just before she came in the room."

The guard rewound the footage to the appropriate time and pressed Play.

Jacobs appeared on the screen, sitting in the chair in front of Percy's room. A tall blonde holding a tray of meds nodded to the constable and walked inside. Seconds later Hudson and Kaylin walked out. After that, the nurse reappeared.

"Wait, freeze it there." Hudson pointed to the frame.

The guard pressed Pause.

The woman's face froze on the screen.

Hudson snapped his fingers. "Got you. Can you send me that frame?" He passed him a card. "To this email address. Now can you let the footage run again? Let's see where she went."

The guard pressed Play. The woman rushed down the corridor and took the door through to the stairs. The camera picked her up on another screen. She was in the east side of the hospital. She hurried around a corner and into a room. She came out as a redhead and in civilian clothes.

Kaylin whistled. "That's how she escaped. She changed and got rid of her wig. See if you can find her anywhere else."

They followed the footage and caught her again leaving the hospital through the front door.

Jacobs cursed. "She left too easily."

Hudson agreed. "Jacobs, go find her wig and clothes. We might be able to get something off them."

He nodded. "I'll take it to Forensics and they'll get back to you." He rushed out of the room.

Hudson's cell phone rang. He swiped the screen. Bianca.

"Steeves here. What do you have, Bianca?"

"A print from Blaine Ridley's apartment."

"Whose?"

"Benji Rossiter. The kid you arrested yesterday. You best get over to his place."

"What?" Hudson's jaw dropped. "We're on our way."

Kaylin gritted her teeth. How did this kid fool them? He had seemed so willing to help them in order to get off any charges. Why would he risk that opportunity? "This doesn't make sense. What was he looking for?"

Hudson shrugged and motioned her toward the elevator. "No idea, but we need to find him. We'll check the Rossiter house first."

"I'm certain his father is going to stonewall us. He wasn't on board before."

"Agreed. We need him to help us convince Benji to give us the truth."

Fifteen minutes later Kaylin exited the cruiser at the Rossiter home. She gazed at the mansion before her. The two-story red brick building housed a four-car garage. A sparkling red Porsche was parked in the driveway. Obviously, Mr. Rossiter came from money, so why did Benji stoop to selling drugs? Kaylin scratched her head. Nothing about this made sense. There had to be more to his story.

Hudson put on his hat, pushed his shoulders back and walked up the concrete driveway, looking like a man on a mission. His resolve to get to the bottom of this mystery was obvious.

She admired the handsome constable even though he

annoyed her at times. He'd mellowed since the last case they'd worked on. His bossy attitude was almost nonexistent now. They had earlier butted heads more times than she could count. It had gotten to the point where they almost didn't catch Jake because they couldn't work together. She shoved her thoughts away and followed Hudson up the front steps.

He rang the bell.

The double oak doors opened and a butler smiled. "May I help you, Officers?"

Hudson tipped his hat. "Yes, we're looking for Benji Rossiter. Is he in?"

The butler glanced over his shoulder and back again. "I'm not sure."

Kaylin stepped forward. "Can you check? It's of vital importance we speak with him."

"I'll see—"

"Rupert, who is it?" David Rossiter pushed the butler aside and stepped into the doorway. His expression tightened. "You two again? What do you want? Haven't you already caused enough damage?"

Hudson's arms stiffened at his side. "Our investigation is ongoing and we have more questions for Benji."

"Hasn't he already sacrificed enough?"

Kaylin sensed more had gone on between this father and son after the takedown. But what? "Sir, we only need a few moments of his time. Is your wife home? Perhaps we could speak to all of you at once."

"It's just the two of us. She's deceased." The man crossed his arms, his body language clearly depicting he was done with this conversation. He eased the door shut.

Hudson stuck his foot in the way. "You have two options. Let us question him here or we'll have to take him into the station."

"Do you have a warrant?"

"We can get one, but do you really want to go over this again?"

Mr. Rossiter swore and opened the door. "Fine, but you only have five minutes." He went to the stairs. "Benji, get your butt down here. Now." His voice roared throughout the massive home.

Their footsteps echoed in the Victorian-style foyer. The tile floor sparkled in the sunlight beaming in from the window at the end of the hall. The kitchen stood off to the right, but Mr. Rossiter led them to the living room. The modern room lay spotless, leaving Kaylin to surmise that this residence also housed a full-time housekeeper. Nothing but the best for the Rossiter family.

Benji bounded down the circular stairs, headphones blaring out music.

"Turn that off and get in here," Mr. Rossiter said as he sat in an oversize cushioned chair. "Benji, what did you do now that warrants a visit from our city's finest?"

Kaylin noticed Hudson's raised brow at Mr. Rossiter's sarcasm.

Benji's eyes widened and he plunked himself onto the sofa. "Don't know."

Hudson sat in a wingback chair. "I think you probably do." He leaned forward. "What were you doing at Blaine Ridley's apartment?"

"I wasn't there."

Kaylin paced. "Then why were your fingerprints all over it? What were you looking for?"

Benji played with his headphones. "I don't need to tell you anything. I know my rights."

Like father, like son. These two were impossible. Trying to get information out of this young lad was like paddling against the current. They were getting nowhere.

She'd try a different tactic. "Do you want your sentence lengthened? Tell us what we need to know, and we may not add this to your list of offenses."

Benji eyed his father.

Mr. Rossiter scowled and twirled his university ring on his finger. "Son, tell them the truth. What were you doing there, and who is Blaine Ridley?"

Benji stood and walked to the window. "He's someone...someone I met during a drug exchange. One of my suppliers."

Kaylin sensed the kid's fear in his shaky voice. He was scared of something. "Why didn't you tell us about him before?"

"Because he told me he'd kill me and I believed him."

Hudson walked to the window and placed his hand on the boy's shoulder. "We'll keep you safe, Benji. What were you looking for at his apartment? Why trash it?"

Benji spun around. "What? I did no such thing. He confiscated a journal I had of my drug sales. I just wanted it back, but I swear I only looked in his drawers. That's all."

If he didn't ransack Blaine's apartment, then who did? Kaylin glanced at Hudson.

He raised his brow. Seems like he had the same question. Instead, he asked, "How did you meet Blaine?"

"He took over from another seller. That was when he wanted my journal."

So there was more to the kid's business than he'd shared yesterday. "Why did he do that?" Kaylin sat on the other end of the plush sofa.

"He was angry I wrote down all my buys. Names, dates, everything. Said they wouldn't like it."

"They?"

Benji shrugged. "That's all I know. I promise."

Hudson stared out the window. The sun's rays shone through and he squinted. "Did you find the journal?"

"Yes."

"We're gonna need that," Hudson said.

"Why?" Benji rubbed the back of his neck.

Kaylin noticed his body language shift. What would be revealed from this journal that he didn't want them to find? "There could be valuable information in it for us. Names and dates that could coincide with drug busts or cross-border shipments."

Benji glanced at his father. Was he looking for his approval?

Mr. Rossiter stood. "Get it for them, Benji. You're done with all that drug nonsense, so you don't need it. Okay, Officers, you got what you wanted. Time to go."

Was Benji telling them everything this time or would they find out he was lying? Kaylin wasn't sure. He seemed to be truthful but she still got a bad vibe from him and his father. Could it just be a bad relationship?

*Kaylin, not every father is like yours.*

Benji left and returned moments later, handing the journal to Hudson. The frown on his face told Kaylin that he didn't want to part with it. That he still planned on selling drugs even after they'd busted him. Why wouldn't he learn?

They exited the mansion and she opened the cruiser's door.

A black F-150 swerved up the driveway, blocking their path. The truck's doors opened. Two masked men emerged and pointed an MP5 submachine gun in their direction.

Her heartbeat quickened.

Hudson and Kaylin reached for their weapons but a voice called out, "Don't move." The taller of the two men stepped forward. "We only want her." He pointed the barrel of his gun in Kaylin's direction.

She raised her arms, her shallow breath catching in her throat. How did they find her?

Hudson's head pounded not only from his migraine, but from the perilous situation at hand. How did these men know where to find them? They hadn't been followed to the Rossiter residence. He kept his hand on the Smith & Wesson still holstered at his hip. "Who are you and what do you want with Kaylin?"

"None of your concern, Constable. Take your hand off that gun of yours." He stepped closer, raising his rifle higher. "Or she and your nephew die."

*Wait. What?* How did they know about Matthew? Hudson obeyed while he racked his mind for a solution that wouldn't get anyone hurt. He lifted his hands in surrender but inched closer to one of the assailants. "Tell us what you want."

A sneer peeked out from behind the man's mask. "I told you. He wants her."

"He?"

Kaylin's gaze met his, her eyes clouded.

"The boss."

Could he mean Valentino? "Look, you don't have to do this. Surrender and we'll take that into—"

The mansion's front door opened and David stepped out. "Hey, what's going on here? Get off my property."

The masked man jerked his weapon in David's direction.

David halted at the sight of drawn machine guns, raising his hands. "Whoa."

It was enough of a distraction to act. Both Kaylin and

Hudson whipped out their weapons, crouching behind the back of the cruiser.

"Get back in the house, Mr. Rossiter," Hudson said, then he turned back to the gunman. "Give it up, man. You won't get away with this."

The silent masked man fired in their direction, bullets spraying the area.

Kaylin and Hudson shot back.

A bullet tore into the first man's leg. He yelled and gripped his thigh, stumbling backward.

"It's over," Hudson said.

The other man fired. "Come on, Blaine. It's not worth it."

Blaine?

The men scrambled into the truck and screeched out of the driveway, racing down the street.

Hudson jumped into the cruiser. "Get in!"

She obeyed and he pulled out after them. He radioed for backup and supplied their location.

The F-150 turned right into the noon rush hour traffic and cut off other cars. Horns blared as vehicles swerved to get out of the truck's path.

Hudson followed with his siren blaring and lights flashing. "You okay?" he asked Kaylin, keeping his eyes on the road.

"I don't understand how they found me."

His hands tightened on the wheel. "I don't know." An overwhelming urgency to protect her punched him in the gut, catching him off guard. "Turn off your cell phone. Just in case."

She pressed the power button.

The truck barreled through a stoplight, barely missing a car. The driver slammed on the brakes and swerved in front of a CRV. Metal screeched as other vehicles rammed into the Honda, effectively blocking their pursuit.

Hudson braked, and Kaylin lurched forward from the motion.

He banged the steering wheel. Another lead lost. He grabbed his radio and reported their position and the direction the F-150 had fled. Other officers would continue with the chase. He requested EMS to the scene.

Two hours later, Hudson sat across from Kaylin at a local Tim Horton's coffee shop. He entered a report on the masked men and pursuit into his company laptop. Paperwork. Part of the job he hated. Took too much time. Time he didn't have right now. How did the masked men know about his nephew? Were they watching him, too?

He took a sip of his dark roast coffee and studied Kaylin. Her slender fingers shook as she traced an entry in Benji's journal. He reached over and placed his hand on top of hers, liking how it felt.

He jolted. No, he couldn't go there. He drew back. "You okay?"

She eyed his reaction and pinched her brows together. "I'm fine." She tapped her thumb on the book. "I had a thought. What if someone else knew about this journal and they also broke into Blaine's apartment to look for it? Benji said he didn't ransack it. What if the next person did? Did the Ident team find any other prints?"

"Bianca only told me about Benji's. Let me check." He pulled out his phone and selected her number. Anything to distract him from this beautiful woman before him.

"What can I do for you, Hudson?" Bianca's voice held an irritation to it.

"Sorry to bother you. Can you tell me if the team found any other prints in the apartment apart from Benji's?" He held his breath in anticipation of some good news.

"There was another full print, but we haven't been able to find a match for it on CPIC."

Figured. Another dead end. "Anything from the van?"

"We scoured the back of it but came up empty."

"What about who it was registered to?" Hudson took a bite of his apple fritter. The freshness melted in his mouth.

He heard papers rustling. "DJ's Florist on Walker Road."

He grabbed his notebook and wrote it down. "Thanks. We'll check it out."

Kaylin dunked her tea bag in her cup. "Nothing?" she asked when he ended the call.

"Nope, just the name of the florist that owned the van. Ident found another print, but no matches."

His phone dinged, announcing an email. He hit a key and forwarded it to Bianca. "Got the nurse's picture from the security guard. I sent it to Bianca. Maybe she can get a hit."

"Hopefully."

An employee turned on the TV above the fireplace. The news appeared on the screen. Images of a recent fire flashed in the background with a female reporter on location.

"Let's look at this journal," Kaylin told him, diverting her attention from the muted TV. "What do you see?" She leaned forward at the same time he did. They bumped heads and held each other's gaze.

Hudson smiled.

She pulled away, glanced at the TV and then back to him.

He cleared his throat and drew his attention away from her, reminding himself that he had a case to solve. He flipped through the pages of the journal. "Names, dates and amounts of Benji's exchanges with these dealers. Plus the type of drug."

"Anything stick out to you?"

He ran his finger down the entries. "I see Blaine's name in here a few times. Many others but no Valentino or Percy. Yesterday could have been their first meet."

"Do you recognize any of the names?" Kaylin leaned closer again and peered at the journal. A strand of hair escaped her ponytail.

He reached out and tucked it behind her ear.

A small gasp escaped her lips.

Did he really just do that?

He brushed it off and pointed to an entry. "Some from past drug arrests."

"How far back do the dates go?"

He turned more pages. "Couple years. Seems Benji has been selling for a while."

"I thought doda was only on the rise now?"

"It's been out there for years, but it just recently became more prevalent." He checked the entries. "Looks like he's been dealing it for a year. Before that it was heroin."

Kaylin finished her tea. "I sure hope Benji gets out of selling and doing drugs. He's a smart kid. His father—" She eyed the TV and he noticed her face blanch.

Hudson grabbed her arm. "What is it?"

Tears welled in her eyes as she pointed to the news report on the TV. "My father is in danger. That's his station."

# SEVEN

Kaylin focused on the news broadcast. The hairs on her arms stood at attention. A police report flashed on the screen along with her father's picture in the corner. Yellow caution tape flapped in the breeze outside the Windsor police station as the female reporter spoke into her microphone. Kaylin bolted out of her chair. Its crash echoed in the small coffee shop, causing other patrons to turn in her direction.

She ignored them and read the caption running across the screen.

WINDSOR POLICE CHIEF MARSHALL POIRIER ATTEMPTED ABDUCTION FOILED.

What?

Hudson stood, eyes peeled to the TV.

Sweat beaded on Kaylin's forehead and a wave of nausea rose in her throat. She swallowed to ward it off and went to raise the volume on the TV in order to hear the blonde reporter.

"Sources tell us that the police chief barely escaped as two masked men tried to abduct him when he pulled in front of the station thirty minutes ago."

Could it be the same men who had tried to snatch her?

She didn't know Hudson had approached her till he grazed her fingers. "He's okay."

She snatched her hand away. "I have to call him." She rushed to the washroom and into a stall. Tears spilled down her cheeks. Why the sudden emotion over the father she barely tolerated?

*He's the only family you have left.*

Thoughts raced through her mind as her head spun. She placed a hand on each wall to steady herself. Her breath came in rapid bursts as her pulse raced. Fast. Faster. She couldn't stop it. The memories rolled in like tumbleweed through a deserted town. Her lip quivered as a scene flashed before her.

"Daddy, I got a B-minus, not an F. Why are you mad at me?" Her ten-year-old fingers crunched the test paper in her hands.

Her father's eyes narrowed. "You can do better."

"But, Daddy, I did my best." Tears threatened to spill from her eyes.

His face reddened. "Are you disagreeing with me, little girl?"

She bit her lip but stayed silent.

"No daughter of mine will be so worthless as to get a B-minus."

She raised her chin. "Don't you love me, Daddy?"

"Why, you ungrateful—" He grabbed the paper and tore it in two.

Why did she have to ask that question? She knew better than to get him mad. Lately, it seemed like it didn't take much. Nothing she did was good enough.

After that episode, she never asked her father again if he loved her. Oh, he had tried to make amends for his verbal abuse, but she found it hard to forgive him. Even after he finally acknowledged her success in the CBSA.

Despite memories like that one, she still needed to find out if he was okay. She turned her cell phone back on and punched in his number.

"Hey, Pumpkin. Don't worry, I'm all right."

Kaylin pulled her shoulders back and lifted her head. "Did you catch them?"

"No. I couldn't ID them, either, but one had a bandaged leg."

The masked man Hudson had shot. "They tried to grab me earlier, too."

"What? Why didn't you tell me?"

Kaylin wiped her eyes and stepped out of the stall. Why hadn't she? "I got too busy." Not a good excuse. "Why are they targeting us?"

"It has to be because I vowed to get rid of drug smugglers." He sighed. "I need to take you off this case. You're not equipped for this."

She cringed. Why couldn't he trust in her abilities? "Dad, I know what I'm doing and I have Hudson. He's a good officer."

"Not enough."

"Trust me. I'll get to the bottom of this. I promise."

There was no running. She would face the ring head-to-head, if need be. After all, she was stronger than that ten-year-old who got a B-minus. Smarter, too. He would not take her off this case.

After what seemed an eternity, he blew out a breath and relented. "Keep me updated. Stop these guys. Fast." Then he clicked off.

That was it? He couldn't tell her he loved her?

Again.

Well, she'd prove to him she could bring this ring down.

Nothing would stand in her way. Not even her father.

Hudson's knee bounced as he waited for Kaylin. What was taking her so long?

*Lord, be with her.*

He sipped his coffee, and by the time he finished, Kaylin returned. Her eyes were glossed over, but in her expression he noted resolve. Determination. "How is your father?"

"As ornery as ever." She opened Benji's journal. "Shall we get back to it? What else did Bianca say?"

Hudson noticed how quickly she wanted to move on. She was off. Withdrawn. But he knew better than to press. If she wanted to share, she'd do it. Maybe she just needed time to trust him. "The owner of the van is DJ's Florist. Shall we go pay them a visit? Snoop around?"

She stood. "Sounds good to me."

"Make sure you turn your cell phone off again. Just in case you're being tracked." He threw his coffee cup in the trash.

Moments later they parked in front of DJ's Florist on Walker Road. Potted daisies, mums and roses lined the sidewalk, inviting customers to peruse and come into the establishment. A white van sat in the driveway. Same make and model as the torched one. Hudson held open the shop's door for Kaylin. The bells chimed, announcing their presence.

Kaylin bent to smell a bucket of yellow roses. "These are my favorites. They make me smile every time I see them."

Maybe he'd buy her some. One day.

He tossed the thought away and studied the small shop. Buckets containing various flowers were placed throughout the store and beautiful arrangements lined the shelves of the cooler. Shoppers filled the tiny space as they picked through the merchandise.

Hudson pointed to the front. "Let's see what we can learn from the florist."

The florist was a petite brunette in her midforties. As

they approached her, she stooped over to grab a daisy. She clipped the bottom and stuck it in the arrangement she worked on. She stood back and eyed her creativity. Obviously satisfied, she grabbed another flower.

Kaylin stepped to the counter. "Morning, ma'am. Can you help us?"

The woman startled at the sight of them and eyed them up and down. She wiped her forehead with the back of her gloved hand.

"What can I do for you, Officers?" Her lips slowly curled into a smile.

Hudson withdrew his badge from his pocket and introduced himself and Kaylin.

Kaylin produced her credentials. "We have some questions for you."

"What could I possibly help you with? I'm just a florist struggling to make a living." She studied the flower arrangement she'd been working on.

*She's hiding something.*

Hudson was sure of it.

Kaylin stepped closer to the woman. "You can tell us why someone shot at us from one of your vans when they attempted to cross the border."

The woman's head snapped back, eyes bulging. "What? Impossible."

"Are you down a van?" Hudson fingered the arrangement she'd been working on. "Some employees?"

She scratched her head. "I've been waiting for my latest shipment and haven't heard back from the driver. I figured he decided to stay overnight in Detroit."

What? She didn't keep track of her delivery workers? Hudson pulled out his phone and flipped to a picture of Akio. "This your driver?"

"Yes. Where is he?"

"Dead. Taken out by a sniper." Kaylin leaned on the counter as she studied the woman's face.

"What?" the florist exclaimed. "Why would anyone kill him?"

"You tell us, ma'am." Hudson paused. "What's your name?"

"Colleen Oliver."

Kaylin stood tall. "Do you own this place?"

The woman nodded. "My husband Lyle and I do. Have for fifteen years. Named our shop after our two kids. Daniel and Julia."

"Why do you import flowers from the States?" Hudson said.

"We buy exotic flowers from all over the world. Not just the States."

"Why?" Kaylin probed the woman closer. She was good at her job, Hudson thought to himself. Why had he given her such a hard time in their last case?

"Better choices and higher demand. I always follow the necessary steps to get them into the country. Nothing illegal about it."

"Then why did your driver and his partner torch the van?" Kaylin said.

Colleen clenched her jaw. "You need to speak to my husband."

"Is he here?" Hudson read the fear in her face. They had her nervous. Good.

"He should be back from his deliveries now. Let me check." She set her clippers down and exited into a room at the back of the store.

Kaylin picked up a flower and examined it. "Do you think she's hiding information?"

"Her tightened body language indicates she's nervous about something. She knows more than she's letting on.

And what business today doesn't keep track of their drivers? Doesn't make sense." As he spoke, he checked his cell phone for updates from his sister. As of this morning, there had been no change in Matthew's condition. The doctors were losing hope but not Hudson. He trusted God would pull him through. He tucked his phone back into his pocket.

"Agreed. You would think she'd keep a closer eye on her shipments. She seemed genuinely surprised when we told her the van was torched."

Hudson mentally reviewed the details of the case. The driver Akio dead. Blaine Ridley's whereabouts undetermined. Benji involved, but how deep? Benji's father acting suspicious. What tied them all together? It didn't add up. He rubbed his brow. "I don't get what's going on with this case. We have too many moving parts. What does one have to do with the other?"

"We need to find Blaine Ridley. Maybe he holds the key. Or at least more information leading us to Valentino."

Colleen emerged with a plump, dark-haired man with circular rimmed glasses. His frown told Hudson he wasn't happy to see them.

The man wiped his brow. "What can I do for you, Officers? I'm Lyle. My wife says you asked for me?"

Hudson introduced them to the man and shook his hand. "Tell us what you know about your latest shipment. What were you having transported across the border that warranted your employees destroying it?"

Lyle's mouth flew open. "He did not act on my orders. He was simply to pick up the flowers and bring them here. That's all."

Kaylin split her stance. "So why would your driver draw a gun and shoot at me?"

Lyle blinked. "He did what now?"

"You heard me," Kaylin said. "What aren't you telling us?"

Hudson tapped his watch. "Where were you at eight fifteen last night?"

"Why, what happened?"

"Your driver, Akio Lee, was taken out by a sniper. Obviously someone didn't want him talking."

Lyle pushed his glasses further up his nose with a shaky finger. "I was here until closing. Nine thirty. You can check our video cameras. Besides, I've never fired a gun in my life."

Kaylin turned to Colleen. "What about you?"

The woman tilted her head. "You're accusing me of murder?" Her high-pitched voice boomed in the small shop.

Shoppers gawked at her.

She leaned closer and lowered her voice. "That's absurd. I was here with my husband. Just like every night. We close the shop together."

"Then why do you suppose someone wanted Akio out of the way?" Hudson asked.

"No idea. We're only simple florists." Lyle didn't make eye contact with either of them.

Hudson's gut told him there was more to this flower shop than this couple let on. Could they be working with the drug smuggling ring? He pointed to a rear door. "Can we see your back room?"

Lyle folded his plump arms. "That's private. Only employees. Do you have a warrant, Constable Steeves?"

So they were going to play that game. "Well, it looks like we'll have to do just that. Don't take any vacations anytime soon. We still need to talk to you."

Kaylin moved toward the exit as more patrons entered. "One more question. Where can we find Blaine Ridley?"

"Who?" Lyle studied his feet.

*Interesting.*

"The passenger who was in the van with your driver. Doesn't he work for you?" Hudson was tired of this man's attitude.

"Never heard of him. We only hired a driver to go across to the States." The man grabbed a cloth and wiped the counter, pushing cut flower stems onto the floor. "Now if you'll excuse us, we have customers to attend to."

Hudson tipped his hat. "We'll be back."

He put his hand on Kaylin's arm and led her through the door. The midafternoon sun hit him like an open oven. He took a breath and exhaled. "What do you make of that interview?"

"They're definitely hiding something. Do we have enough to get a warrant to search the place?"

"I'm going to try." He fumbled in his pocket for his keys, dropping them on the sidewalk. *Klutz!*

"Where to—"

His cruiser exploded with a thunderous roar.

The blast thrust Kaylin into the front of the building, breaking the window. Glass shattered onto the pavement and sliced into her skin as she fell to the ground. Trickles of blood oozed down her arms. Her head throbbed. The heat from the inferno burned her face and she tried to shield herself. It assaulted her nose. Her pulse raced, bringing a wave of nausea with it. She breathed in. Out. In. Out. She needed to slow her heart rate down. She willed herself to move but couldn't.

Flames torched the cruiser and rose higher into the sky, blanketing the area with smoke. She placed her hand over her mouth to prevent further inhalation. Where was Hudson?

Kaylin shook her head to clear the fogginess. She exhaled. What would have happened if Hudson hadn't dropped his keys? A shudder ran through her body. Could it be God had protected them?

Dare she even consider that? He hadn't been there all her life, so why now? Surely it was just a coincidence.

She placed her bloody hand on the rough pavement and eased herself up. "Hudson?"

Silence.

The constable lay a few feet away. He'd been thrown down the sidewalk.

She stumbled over to him. "Hudson? Can you hear me?"

Nothing.

She swayed and grabbed the side of the building to steady herself. Once the wave of dizziness passed, she knelt beside him. "Hudson, talk to me." She turned him over.

Blood caked his face.

She checked his pulse. Steady. She shook him. "Hudson, wake up." She reached for her cell phone, but her pocket was empty. She glanced around. It lay shattered on the pavement. Useless.

Colleen and Lyle rushed out of the florist shop. "Are you okay, Officer?"

"He's unconscious and needs help. My phone was damaged. Call 911."

Colleen ran back into the building.

Lyle walked closer to the flaming cruiser and whistled. "Who would have done this?"

Good question. Had they targeted her again?

A crowd formed. Onlookers filled both sides of the streets, trying to catch a glimpse of the event. Was the bomber among them? They said suspects sometimes stayed to watch after they'd committed a crime, as if admiring their handiwork. Did that happen today?

She jumped up and surveyed the expressions on the faces of the onlookers. "Someone bent on preventing us from getting any answers," she finally replied to the florist.

Had the suspect been watching them? If so, why not wait until they were in the vehicle? Then she remembered what was in the cruiser. The journal. Obviously, someone wanted it destroyed. That meant there were incriminating names listed on the pages. She eyed the burning cruiser. All was lost now.

Colleen joined them back out on the street. "EMS, fire rescue and Windsor police are on their way." She looked at the shop. "Our window is destroyed."

Kaylin stopped picking shards of glass out of her hair, her eyes narrowing. "You're worried about your window when Constable Steeves is lying unconscious?"

The woman shrugged and walked back into the shop.

Kaylin's face flushed, and she rubbed her brow. She would never understand how some people reacted in a crisis. She shook her head and crouched beside Hudson. She rubbed his arm. "Come on. Wake up." She couldn't lose him. Not now. He'd raced into her life unexpectedly, taking her by surprise. Even when she had been resolved to steer clear of men.

Sirens sounded in the distance. They drew louder.

Good, they needed to get him to the hospital. "Come on. Come back to us."

Hudson lay still as the blood dripped down the sides of his face.

The ambulance, fire truck and police cruiser pulled up in front of the flaming car. Firemen jumped from their truck and hooked up their hose to a nearby hydrant as EMS workers rushed to Hudson's side.

"What happened, Officer?" one of the technicians asked her as he checked Hudson's vitals.

Kaylin stood. "He was thrown from the blast. I think he hit his head on the pavement."

One paramedic shone a light into both eyes. "His pulse is strong. Could be a concussion. We need to get him to Windsor Regional right away."

Another paramedic approached with a gurney. They eased Hudson onto it and lifted him into the back of the ambulance.

Two police officers canvassed the crowd, asking questions. Another officer approached her. "We'll need to take your statement."

Kaylin shook her head. "Not now. I'm going with him." She nodded toward Hudson in the ambulance.

"You'll need to get checked, as well, ma'am," one of the paramedics interjected as he walked by.

The officer stepped back. "Then we'll meet you at the hospital after we talk to the others here." He nodded toward the florist shop's owner.

"Sounds good." She willed her weakened legs to step into the back of the ambulance. The situation had stressed her more than she realized. Would Hudson be okay? She sent up a quick prayer.

Would God hear her after all of the negativity she had toward Him?

An hour later, after getting checked out at the hospital, she sat by Hudson's bedside. He still hadn't regained consciousness. She studied his cell phone, which she'd removed from his pocket. Whom should she call? Where was his mother? A girlfriend? The thought of a woman in his life somehow stung. Why did it bother her so much? To think she couldn't stand his cocky attitude six months ago. What had changed? Or perhaps he had simply warmed up to her.

She eyed the handsome officer. Nurses had washed the blood from his face and bandaged his cuts. Kaylin had cringed at the amount covering his cheeks. The laceration on his forehead had to be stitched due to the depth of it. No wonder the blast had knocked him unconscious. She sat beside the bed and took Hudson's hand, rubbing his fingers. Why did she want to get to know this man all of a sudden?

His cell phone buzzed.

A gorgeous redhead's face popped up on his screen with a name above it.

Rebecca.

Kaylin bit her lip. Should she answer?

She hit the Talk button. "Officer Poirier here."

"Who? Where's Hudson?"

"Can I ask who's calling?"

"Rebecca. His fiancée."

Kaylin froze.

# EIGHT

Hudson licked his cracked lips and swallowed. His parched throat longed for water. He opened his eyes and blinked several times to clear the fogginess in his throbbing head and get accustomed to the bright lights. He touched the bump on his forehead and moaned. Where was he? Why did his entire body feel like a cement truck had hit him?

Wait. The blast.

Where was Kaylin?

He bolted upright, but immediately regretted it as a wave of nausea slammed him. He eased back down and took big breaths until the feeling subsided.

The smell of rubbing alcohol filled the small room. Beeping noises sounded from outside his door. He was in a hospital. Windsor Regional.

He looked around the room and found Kaylin asleep in a chair beside him. How long had he been here?

Who blew up his cruiser?

Questions raced through his mind, but he was only concerned about the beautiful woman sitting next to him. Relieved she was okay, he took her hand.

She startled. "You're awake."

"Were you worried about me, Officer Poirier?" He winked.

She smiled mischievously. "What do you think?"

"How long have I been out?" He eased himself up. He had to get out of here and back on the case. It wouldn't solve itself. If he didn't, he'd never hear the end of it from his boss.

"Five hours."

"Tell me what happened."

She rubbed her hand over the armrest. "The blast threw us both. Thankfully you stopped to pick up your keys. I think that saved our lives."

"It was all God."

She shifted in her chair, her unbelief evident on her contorted face. "Not sure I believe that."

"It's the only answer, Kaylin. He made me fumble with my keys and drop them. That's not something I normally do." Why did she have such a hard time believing?

She shrugged. "Well, I'm not so sure. Why did He allow it to happen in the first place?"

How could he make her understand? "Listen, I don't have all the answers. I just know He loves me. You, too."

She bit her lip and looked away.

Clearly something had happened in the past to steer her from a loving God. Would she ever tell him what it was?

*I want to know more about you, Kaylin.*

He cleared his throat. Time to change the subject. "What have the authorities said about the bombing?"

"They questioned me here at the hospital and I gave them my statement, which wasn't much to go on." She leaned in, resting her elbows on the bed. "How did they know where we were to get access to your car?"

He raised the bed and eased himself up. "I don't know, but we've obviously struck a nerve with someone." His head pounded. He needed some of his migraine medication to stop it from getting worse.

Kaylin suddenly sat back and crossed her arms over her middle.

He studied her tight expression. Was it anxiousness or fear showing on her pretty face? "What are you thinking?"

She twirled a ring around her finger. "This is all my fault. They're targeting me. Maybe Dad is right. I should remove myself from this task force."

"You can't."

"Why?"

"Because we're getting closer and we need you. You're determined and capable." He lowered the railings and swung his legs over the side. "I need my phone." It was time to get moving. He couldn't lie around all day.

She jumped up and stood in front of him. "Get back into bed. You're in no condition to be leaving this hospital."

Their eyes locked for a moment. Why did he have the sudden urge to take her in his arms and tell her everything would be okay? He shook his head to clear the image rolling through his brain. Where did that come from? She was messing with his head. *Hudson, focus. You don't need to fall for another woman.* He would not surrender to those chocolate brown eyes.

He looked away to break his concentration. "I need to call my sergeant to get you protection. Twenty-four/seven."

She pushed him back into the narrow hospital bed. "You're not going anywhere, and I can take care of myself." She handed him his cell phone. "But you can have this back. Your fiancée called."

The disdain in her voice revealed the reason for her sudden mood change.

He blinked. "My who?"

"You know, Rebecca." Her lips flattened.

"She's not—"

"I gotta run and get a new cell phone since mine was

destroyed. Talk to you later, okay?" She rushed from the room before he had a chance to explain.

His cell phone buzzed. His boss. "Hey, Sarge."

"How are you feeling? I heard about the bombing."

"My head throbs."

"Just wanted to let you know they found the trigger. Looks like remote detonation. They were watching you."

Chills danced along his skin, forming goose bumps. Someone had indeed targeted them.

Now they were in more danger.

He needed to call Kaylin.

But how? She didn't have a cell phone.

Kaylin spotted a man wearing a baseball cap low over his eyes. He stood behind a column in the cellular store, watching her. She felt a chill at the back of her neck. Was he following her? She stepped away from the counter and circled around him. He moved to a kiosk and fingered the phones, keeping his head dipped. Seconds later he exited the store.

She let out the breath she didn't realize she'd been holding and stepped to the counter and pointed to a cell phone to purchase, giving the clerk her information.

An hour later, she arrived back at her apartment and looked right, then left before inserting her key into the lock. She couldn't shake the feeling that someone was watching her, but there hadn't been a tail on her drive home. She circled her subdivision just in case. And an officer was camped outside her building. Again.

*Get a grip.*

She walked inside her two-bedroom apartment, placed her keys on the foyer table and removed her gun before locking it in her hidden safe. She had received special permission to bring her weapon home and she couldn't be too careful.

Sassme greeted her by rubbing around her legs. Kaylin scooped the cat up and snuggled into her soft fur. It tickled Kaylin's nose. "Hey, girl. You hungry?"

The cat meowed as if in agreement.

"Okay." She carried her pet into the kitchen and set her on the floor before filling the dish with food.

Her mind raced back to Hudson. They'd had a moment in his hospital room. She struggled with feelings she never thought she'd have for someone again.

*Stop it. He'd never go for you.*

She had too much baggage and she'd have to share more than she wanted to.

And besides, he had Rebecca.

Kaylin needed to get her mind off him. Perhaps a call to her friend was in order. She turned her cell phone back on and selected her best bud's number. Hannah Morgan now lived in Whitehorse, Yukon, patrolling the border along Yukon and Alaska.

Hannah answered on the third ring.

"Hey, friend. It's me. Good to hear your voice. I miss you." Kaylin had met Hannah on the streets of Windsor and they'd both ended up living with Diane. Hannah was the sister Kaylin never had. They'd been inseparable during her high school years and had also gone to CBSA college together.

"How's it going at the Windsor-Detroit border?"

"Interesting. Dad has ordered me to work on a doda drug smuggling ring with police officer Hudson Steeves." Kaylin moved into her bedroom and plunked herself on the bed.

"Him again? Didn't you have issues with him on Jake's case?"

"Yes. He seems different this time, though. Kinder."

Hannah whistled. "Do I hear admiration in your voice?"

Kaylin removed the radio from her shoulder. "Maybe." She grabbed her pajamas from a drawer and headed to the bathroom. "Doesn't matter, though. He has a fiancée." The contempt in her voice surprised even herself. Had she developed a crush on the constable in only two days?

"You sound bitter."

"Just tired." Tired of being targeted. She pulled a towel and washcloth out of her linen closet, dropping them on the bathroom vanity. "What are you working on?"

"We're having issues of children being kidnapped and smuggled across different border crossings between Yukon and Alaska. I guess they're putting together a task force to deal with it."

"Will you be on it?"

"I hope so. It breaks my heart. All those kids torn from their families. For what? To work in sweatshops?"

"Sad."

"How's your dad?"

She walked back into the living room and flipped on her TV. The newscast replayed her father's attempted abduction. Sassme jumped on her lap, circled a few times and then lay down. Kaylin buried her fingers in the cat's fur. Its softness soothed her. "The same."

"You need to forgive, my friend. It's what God wants."

Kaylin huffed. "You sound like Diane."

"It's true. God is calling to you. Surrender your life to Him."

"Oh. Guess what? Hudson is a Christian, too. I'm surrounded."

Hannah laughed. "Good, maybe he can knock some sense into you."

Kaylin kicked her feet up on the coffee table, disturbing Sassme, who scurried out of the room. "I doubt it."

"Kaylin, the bitterness is holding you back from a life of freedom. You need peace and the only way you'll get it is through forgiveness."

She pinched the bridge of her nose, trying to ward off a tension headache. "How can you say that after knowing what my father did to me?"

"I know it's hard, but living the way you are is eating you up. He's trying to make amends."

Kaylin couldn't listen to her friend anymore. She didn't understand. It wasn't that easy to forget the past. "Listen, I gotta run. Good chatting with you. Talk again next week?"

Hannah sighed. "Sure. Sorry if I overstepped my bounds. I only want the best for you."

"I know. Love you."

"You, too, my friend. Bye."

Kaylin hung up and snapped off the TV. She texted Hudson and let him know her new number.

Within moments, her cell phone buzzed with a message from Hudson.

Tks 4 ur new #.

NP. How r u feeling?

Better. Sarge says bomb set off by remote. Be careful.

Will do. Nite.

C u 2moro.

Kaylin walked to her bathroom, tossed her cell phone on the vanity table and grabbed her hairbrush. She pulled the elastic from her ponytail and massaged her head. The blast had thrown her and now she was feeling it. She rubbed her arms where the glass had sliced her skin. Was that just a few hours ago? The long day had taken its toll and she needed sleep.

Sassme trotted into the room and jumped up on the vanity, watching her with wide eyes.

Kaylin rubbed the cat's head before squirting toothpaste onto her toothbrush. She turned on the faucet.

*Creak.*

She paused. What was that?

*Creak.*

She snapped the faucet off and listened.

Drawers opened and closed in her bedroom.

She clamped her hand over her mouth and grabbed Sassme, squeezing her tight. Someone was in her apartment.

And her gun was locked away in another room.

# NINE

Hudson thrashed about, exhaustion consuming his battered body. He tried to get into a comfortable position on the narrow bed but wasn't successful. He wanted to go home and crawl into his own comfy bed, but the doctor wanted him kept overnight for observation. If all was well in the morning, they'd release him. He couldn't get out of there quick enough. His sister had visited him earlier and given him an update on Matthew. Nothing new.

Hudson thought back on the events of the past few days. Their investigation into this drug ring was obviously getting closer and the team's lives were at stake. If not, then why bomb his cruiser and destroy the only evidence they had of a drug smuggling ring? The journal was lost in the flames.

*Why, God? Can't You give us a clue as to where this ring originates?*

His cell phone buzzed on the night table. Kaylin.

He sat upright. Why would she be calling this late? "Kaylin, what's wrong?"

"Someone's in my apartment," she whispered.

He flung the covers off and jumped out of bed. Dizziness overwhelmed him, so he braced himself against the wall to let it pass. "Where are you?"

"Locked in the bathroom. My gun is in the other room. I've called 911. The officer stationed outside should be here any moment."

*Lord, protect her.*

"Text me your address. I'll be right there."

"Be careful. They might be after you, too." She clicked off.

He changed his clothes and called for a car as he ran out of the room and down the corridor.

The nurse at the station yelled. "Where do you think you're headed, Mr. Steeves?"

"Emergency. I'll be back."

She frowned. "You shouldn't leave."

He ignored her and kept running. He had to protect the woman he'd grown to care about so quickly. The thought raced by him without him even noticing.

A few minutes later, he rushed out of the Uber in front of Kaylin's apartment. Out of habit he reached for his sidearm, but it wasn't there. How would he keep her safe?

The front door was propped open and he raced up the stairs to the second floor. He checked the numbers as he ran by.

289. The door was ajar, lock broken. He eased it open and almost tripped over something in the darkened room. The only glow came from the moonlight shining through the window.

A Windsor police officer was face-down on the floor.

Hudson knelt and felt for a pulse. Steady. *Thank You, Lord.*

A shadow skulked by the living room entrance.

Hudson straightened. Had the intruder done anything to Kaylin? He stood and forced himself to concentrate, tightening his fists for battle since he didn't have his gun. He wouldn't let anything happen to her. "Police! Stop!"

A man barreled through, knocking over a chair and an end table.

Hudson reached out to grab him, but the beefy figure shoved him out of the way. Hudson caught a glimpse of the man wearing night goggles.

Hudson turned on the lights and the room flooded with brightness.

The man yelled and removed his goggles. He fumbled for the door and swung it open, racing out into the hall.

Hudson returned to the downed officer and gently shook him.

The officer moaned and rubbed his head.

Hudson pulled out his credentials. "Constable Hudson Steeves. You okay?" He helped the man sit up.

The bald officer nodded.

"Can I borrow your radio?"

He pulled it off his shoulder and handed it to Hudson.

Hudson spoke into it, identifying himself. He explained the situation and asked for additional units to search for the suspect, giving them a brief description. Of what he saw of him anyway. "We also need an ambulance at the victim's apartment. Your officer is injured." He gave the necessary details and clicked off.

"Where's Miss Poirier?" the officer asked. "The attacker knocked me out before I could get to her."

Hudson ran to the bathroom. "Kaylin? Are you in there?" He turned the doorknob. Locked. "Kaylin?"

The door swung open and she collapsed into his arms. "Thank God you're here."

A cat hissed and sprang out of the room.

Hudson held her tight. "I've got you. He's gone."

She exhaled, air whooshing through her teeth. "Did you see his face? Who was it?"

He shook his head. "He got away. We've called for backup. The assailant knocked out the officer." He released her. "Are you okay?"

"It sounded like he was looking for something." She hurried into the bedroom.

Overturned drawers lay on the floor with clothes

strewn about the room. The covers were ripped off her bed and the table lamp knocked over.

"What was he searching for?" Kaylin took a step, but Hudson pulled her back.

"Wait. We need Ident down here to check for prints. Don't touch anything." He pulled out his cell phone and called Bianca, asking for the forensic unit.

Kaylin wandered into the living room.

He followed, not letting her out of his sight.

"I can't believe he got through my locks." Kaylin massaged her neck.

"Obviously, a professional. Did you notice anyone following you tonight after you left the hospital?"

"No one followed me home. But I saw a man in a ball cap watching me at the phone store, but then he left, so I thought it was my overactive imagination."

"How tall?"

She chewed on her lower lip. "About six-four. Heavyset."

"Sounds like the same guy. Anything else?"

"No."

"Do you have a place where you can stay tonight? I don't want you to be alone." He wouldn't take that chance again. Not when she'd been targeted. Definitely not on his watch. "Your dad's?"

"No. I can call my friend, Diane. I used to live with her."

"Good." He walked to the window and turned. "I'll see if—"

He stopped. An object on the foyer table caught his eye. "What's that?"

A decapitated stuffed bear sat in the middle of the table, its head to the side, smothered in a red substance.

Blood?

Kaylin grabbed the table to steady herself. Who was this person and why had they targeted her? She glanced around the damaged living room. The couch was torn to pieces, her TV smashed and books knocked off their shelves. Fear kicked her in the stomach and her hands shook, but she would not buckle. She was stronger than that. Her pulse throbbed in her head. Whoever was doing this would pay. She'd see to it that they be prosecuted to the fullest extent of the law.

Hudson clicked off his call and stepped beside her.

"I want you to arrest whoever did this. It's unaccept-able." She spaced her words slowly, gritting her teeth.

"Agreed. I'm just glad he didn't get to you."

She raised her eyebrow. "Why not force his way into the bathroom? He must have known I was there."

Hudson stroked his five o'clock shadow. "Good ques-tion, but thank God he didn't. Perhaps he only wanted to scare you."

Sassme's bright eyes glowed from under the living room chair. Kaylin pulled her out and snuggled the cat next to her cheek. "It doesn't make any sense. He wouldn't have known I was in the bathroom when he entered."

"He probably figured you were in bed at this hour."

She nodded. "Perhaps."

He scratched the cat's head. "I was worried when I got your call. You sounded frantic."

She stood resolute, ready to take action. "I had a moment of weakness, but I'm okay now. I want to catch this guy."

"I spoke to Bianca. She's on her way with the team to do a full sweep of your apartment. However, I noticed the suspect wore gloves, so I doubt we'll find any prints."

She fingered the cat's paw and then released her to the floor. "Probably not. I can't imagine who did this."

"Can you think of anyone who has a grudge against you?"

She rubbed her eyes. She needed sleep soon or she'd

collapse. "No. It has to be related to this task force. The threatening texts started after it was formed."

Another Windsor police officer knocked on the open door and entered. "Constable, we spotted a suspect running. He matched your description but he got away. He ducked into a nearby bar and blended in with the crowd. Must have slipped out the back."

"Did you put a BOLO out on him?" Hudson asked.

"Yes, although we didn't get the best look at him, so there's not much to go on." He turned to Kaylin. "He hurt you, miss?"

"No, I locked myself in the bathroom and waited for the police." Some strong officer she turned out to be.

"You did the smart thing." The officer's radio crackled, announcing another call across the city. "You contact Forensics, Constable?"

"Yes, they should be here any moment."

A knock sounded at the door and Bianca poked her head in. "Good evening." She and the Forensics team walked in. Paramedics followed and attended to the injured officer.

"That was fast," Hudson told Bianca.

"We were just finishing up at a nearby call. My shift is almost over. What happened here?"

Hudson recalled their encounter with the suspect as the other officer took Kaylin's statement.

Two hours later, the officer left and said they'd contact her if anything came up. He promised to tell Hudson if they got a lead from the BOLO. Paramedics transported the injured officer to the hospital.

Bianca and the team finished their investigation, telling her it was okay to move around her apartment. The substance on the bear was nothing more than ketchup, but the intent was clear.

Kaylin was in danger.

She glanced at the mess. Did she really want to clean this up now? No. Instead, she called Diane and asked if she could stay with her tonight. Just until she could change the locks and get a better security system. Diane agreed to take her and Sassme in.

Kaylin put her cat into a carrying cage and collected some personal items and a clean uniform, along with her gun. Then she turned to Hudson. "Ready? I'll take you back to the hospital."

"I'll get another officer to follow us and ensure we're okay. He'll then tag along to where you're staying. I want you to be safe." He played with one of her curls and his fingers grazed her cheeks.

At the contact, she felt herself flush. The spark between them was undeniable, and she wanted to lean in closer to his touch. Till she remembered the call from Rebecca on his cell phone. No, he was off-limits, and Kaylin wouldn't open her heart again.

"I'll be okay at Diane's. She has a great alarm system."

"I'm not taking any chances. Especially after tonight." He called the Windsor police and made arrangements for an escort. "They'll be here soon."

The cruiser arrived ten minutes later. She grabbed her cat and her bag. "Let's go."

They left the building and Kaylin unlocked her Honda Civic and pulled out of the parking lot with their protection in tow. She eyed Hudson beside her.

He rested his head against the back of the seat and shut his eyes.

She touched his arm. "Your head still bad?"

"It's throbbing again. Guess I need more painkillers. The nurse at the hospital is going to give me a lashing for leaving."

"You shouldn't have come." She shouldn't have called. It was her fault.

He turned his head and smiled. "Wouldn't have it any other way. I needed to be sure you were okay."

He grabbed her hand and squeezed.

Her face flushed again and she snapped her gaze back to the road. She couldn't let him see the effect he had on her. Where was this coming from? She'd vowed to stay clear of men after Jake had broken her heart. She couldn't let Hudson chip away at her armor.

And, of course, he was engaged.

"Tell me about Rebecca. Where did you meet?" She took a right at the intersection and glanced in the rearview mirror. The cruiser followed, but there were no signs of any other tails. They were safe. For now.

He grunted. "At a church picnic. Kind of ironic after how she treated me."

"What do you mean? I thought you were engaged." Was there hope for her?

*Stop it, Kaylin. He's off-limits.*

"Not anymore. She lied. We broke up a year ago. I have no idea why she told you that." He wrung his hands together and his eyes tightened. "She cheated on me with two men."

Kaylin whistled. No wonder he'd had such a lousy attitude back when they'd first started working together on Jake's case. What man would trust any woman after that? "She dated three men at once?"

"I know, right? Unbelievable." He looked out the passenger-side window. "I was in love with her and she broke my heart. That's hard to get over."

Thoughts of Jake filled her mind. She'd fallen fast for him but then paid the ultimate price. Diane told her she needed to forgive him for the pain he'd caused, but she couldn't do it. Even if he did claim he'd turned over a new leaf. Hardly. She'd believed him once and taken him back, only to find out he was dealing drugs. She'd vowed to help put him away. She couldn't have another dealer on the streets. Not after what had happened to her brother.

"You don't think people can change?" Not that she did, either, but he claimed to be a Christian. Surely he believed in redemption?

"Of course, but I don't trust her. I will not let anyone in my heart who holds secrets. Never again."

Kaylin's breath hitched.

She had plenty of secrets and ones she vowed to keep to herself.

Kaylin arrived at Diane's at midnight. She parked the car and waved to the officer across the street. She shook her head. This shouldn't be happening. Who could be targeting her? She racked her brain for any past arrests she'd made at the CBSA, but no one stood out.

The front light illuminated the three-bedroom bungalow. The stars twinkled, and the muggy air had cleared. If it wasn't so late, she would take a long walk. However, after what had transpired in the past couple of days, she didn't feel safe even in this friendly neighborhood. Kaylin picked up her bag and Sassme's carrier before bounding up the steps. She glanced around the yard to see if anyone else was in sight. Satisfied only the crickets lingered, she inserted her key into the lock. She'd lived here for quite a few years and it still felt like home base. Diane was her shelter through all her storms.

She stepped inside expecting silence, but Diane sat at the kitchen table, drinking tea.

"Hey, love." She jumped up and embraced her.

The tiny woman's hugs personified love. Her embrace felt like a haven.

"What are you doing up, Diane? You should be in bed." Kaylin opened the cage and Sassme scurried into the next room.

"You gave me a fright and I had to see you. Are you okay?" Diane sat back down and took a sip.

Kaylin moved to the cupboard and pulled out a cup. She needed some tea to calm her frayed nerves. She turned the kettle on. "I'm fine. Now. It was a bit scary at first when I didn't know if the suspect would bust down the bathroom door or not. Thankfully, the police and Hudson showed up when they did."

"Hudson?"

"Constable Hudson Steeves."

Diane's eyes sparkled in the dim lighting. "Sounds interesting. What does he look like?"

She crossed her arms. "Now you sound like Hannah. I'll admit he's gorgeous, but nothing is going to happen between us. He's a Christian and doesn't like someone with secrets, and I can't tell him my story."

"Why, love? He'll understand."

Kaylin unwrapped a bag of chamomile tea, dropped it in her cup and added hot water. Hopefully it would calm her nerves so she could sleep. "I can't take that chance. Besides, it's none of his business." She wrapped her hands around the warm mug, letting its heat quiet her. If only it would ease her troubled mind.

Diane tilted her head. "It would be good to have a handsome police officer in your court."

"Stop."

"You need to forgive and let God heal your broken heart. You've been through so much with your father and Jake."

Kaylin drank her tea. The flowery flavor tingled her tongue and soothed her dry throat. "I don't need another lecture on God. I'm tired and edgy."

"I wish you could see His love for you."

"Who could love a girl who's lived her life wrapped in

so many secrets? I'm not worthy." Any hope she thought she had with Hudson was gone.

Diane clucked her tongue. "Your father ingrained that into your brain. His lies still reach you after all these years. I thought he'd changed."

Was it true? Did she believe she wasn't worthy of love? First her father and then Jake. No way could she open up to Hudson. Her frail heart couldn't take it.

Or to a God she couldn't see.

Kaylin remained silent. She didn't want to talk about her father. Even though she was concerned for his safety.

Diane put her cup in the sink. "I'm heading to bed. Your room is ready."

"Thanks. See you in the morning."

Diane kissed the top of Kaylin's head. "God loves you and so do I."

"Love you, too."

Diane blew her a kiss and left the room.

Kaylin finished her tea and took the cup to the sink. She breathed in the familiar vanilla scent of this three-bedroom bungalow she'd lived in years ago. She was home. Her shoulders relaxed.

Her cell phone chimed.

She grabbed it from her pocket and swiped the screen.

I saw u with Constable Steeves. Stay away from him. U're mine. XO.

How did they get her new number so quickly? Kaylin turned the GPS off on her phone and threw it on the counter, her muscles tensing. No way would she sleep tonight. She dashed to the window and pulled the drapes.

Was this person watching her right now?

# TEN

Kaylin's cell phone buzzed and she rolled over, glancing at the clock. 7:30 a.m. She'd overslept, even after the threatening text from last night. She checked the caller. Her boss. She sat up quickly. Sassme leaped off the bed and scrambled under it. What happened to warrant a call from her leader so early?

"Morning, Superintendent Thompkins." Her voice did little to hide her morning grogginess. She cleared her throat.

"You sleep in, Poirier?" His rough tone revealed his cranky mood.

*Great. Just what I need.*

"I had an interesting evening last night."

"I heard about the bombing. Why didn't you call me? Had to hear it from Steeves's boss."

She winced. "Sorry, too much going on. What's up?" She twirled a strand of hair between her fingers, dreading the words about to come from his mouth.

"You and Constable Steeves need to get down here right away. We've detained another DJ's Florist van and sequestered the driver."

She jumped out of bed and grabbed her clothes. "Understood. Be there as soon as I can."

"You better. We need to wrap up this case soon." He hung up.

"Ugh." She threw the cell phone on the bed and ran

to the bathroom. First her father and now her boss. Why couldn't they trust in her abilities?

Then again, could she?

Forty-five minutes later, she pulled into the parking lot of the CBSA office at the Windsor-Detroit border. She called Hudson on the way and found out the doctor had released him. He'd be there as soon as he could.

Kaylin spotted the florist van out front as she entered the building. She wanted to get the lowdown from her boss first, so she made her way directly to his office and knocked.

"Come in." His voice boomed through the door.

She steeled her jaw and entered. "Morning, Superintendent Thompkins."

"'Bout time you got here. Where's Steeves?"

"On his way. He just got released from the hospital."

Her boss pulled out a sheet of paper. "Got the police report on the bombing. Says here it was a remote detonation."

"Yes, someone was watching us."

"You know this for sure?"

"I've had an attempted abduction, plus threatening texts."

His eyes narrowed. "Why didn't you tell me this?"

She sat facing his desk. "Sorry. I should have." She hoped he wouldn't let this be the reason to take her off the case. She needed to see this through no matter the cost. She didn't abandon cases. "What time did the florist van come through?"

"Four a.m."

"Why did the security officer stop it?"

"Too much of a coincidence since the shooting a couple days ago. The driver says he's only doing his job, but we need to be sure it's legit." He clicked his computer and leaned in. "Driver's passport is showing Bart Hardy. Has all the right certificate papers."

"Same as the other van. Coincidence?"

"I don't believe in those and that's why you're here. You and Steeves questioned the other driver. You should question this one. He's getting antsy, though, since he's been here a few hours." He sat back in his chair. "Find some answers. Hardy is in interrogation room one. If you don't wrap this case up soon, I'll have to replace you." He steepled his fingers. "Even if your father is the chief of police."

Kaylin stood. She was good at what she did, but her boss never seemed to notice. "We'll get something out of him."

"You'll need these." He handed her the keys to the van.

She rushed out the door and collided with Hudson, falling into his arms. At his touch ripples of pleasure surged up her spine. She imagined what it would be like to stay in his embrace.

*Snap out of it, Kaylin. Remember your secrets.*

She gulped and stepped back. "Morning. You got here fast."

He smiled, his eyes grinning back at her. "We have work to do."

"How are you feeling?"

He rubbed his head. "Little sore, but okay. Did you sleep?"

"Some." She pulled her cell phone out. "Got this text last night."

He whistled. "Let me take your phone to have it checked out. Perhaps our team can trace the text's origin."

"I turned off the GPS. Should have done it sooner." She handed it to him. "I doubt you'll find anything. This person is too smart for that."

"It's worth a try." He nodded over his shoulder. "I saw the florist van outside. Have you checked it out?"

She shook her head. "Do you want to do that before we interrogate the driver?"

Hudson opened the door for her. "Shall we?"

She nodded and pulled gloves out of her pocket.

She stepped outside and the stifling hot air greeted her, robbing her breath. She hated the summer. Too muggy for her liking. Even in June. Fall was her favorite. The colors brought her joy every year. She wiped the perspiration forming on her brow and walked toward the florist van. Using the keys, she unlocked the driver's-side door. "Let's start in the front."

"How many were in the van?"

"Only a driver this time. Not sure why." She opened the glove box and rummaged through the contents. Flashlight, set of pocket-size screwdrivers and vehicle registration papers. She reached in deeper and pulled out another object buried at the back.

A gun.

She held it up, dangling it by the trigger guard. "Look what I found. Seems as if this driver isn't as innocent as he's saying."

Hudson held open a plastic bag and she dumped it inside. "Anything else?"

"I'll check under the seats." She pulled out her flashlight, knelt and shone the light. Nothing stood out to her. She rummaged under the cushion, her hand catching the edge of an item taped to the underside of the seat. She tugged at it, pulling out photos clipped together in a plastic bag.

"What do we have here?" She opened it.

Hudson leaned in. "What is it?"

She caught a whiff of his woodsy scent and inhaled.

*I could get used to his closeness.*

She rubbed her nose to clear the smell and concentrated on the job before her. "Looks like pictures." She thumbed through them and stumbled backward. Pictures of her, Hudson, her father and Diane, with some type of ransom figure written on the back. "What could this mean?"

"Looks like they're targeting the task force and any-one close to them. Good thing we have a protective detail on Diane's house."

Kaylin cringed. She hated that she'd now put her friend in danger. How far would this gang go to disband their task force? She put the photos back in the bag and reached in behind the seat, feeling her way around, but came up empty. She pulled a screwdriver from her pocket and re-moved the door's side panel, examining it carefully, as it was a common place where drugs were stashed. She walked around to the other side and did the same to that door. Nothing.

Hudson moved to the rear of the van. "Time to check out what's inside."

She unlocked the back and opened the double doors.

Buckets of flowers lined every inch of the floor as well as side shelves.

"Okay, this is normal for a florist van. Flowers." The overpowering perfume smell tickled her nose.

"Pull some out. I want to look at them closer."

She brought out a bucket and placed it on the pavement. Irises, roses, daisies, bird of paradise and dried poppies filled it. She pulled out another bucket. That one was the same, except it held more poppies.

Hudson fingered one and lifted it out. The tan-colored dehydrated stem and seed head crumbled in his hand. "Oh, my."

"What?"

"This is how they're getting the drugs into the country. They're using florist's vans filled with dried poppy straw."

"Is that illegal?"

"It's a gray area. There are certain regulations that need to be followed. It appears the florist is disguising the dried poppy straw so people will think they're just part of a flo-ral arrangement, but the pods are crushed into a powder to produce doda. It all looks perfectly legal, but someone is obviously using it for illegal purposes."

"How are they ingested?"

"The powder is used to make tea or simply stirred into a glass of water or drink."

She stiffened her arms at her sides. "We need to talk to that driver. Now."

"My guess is that's why the other van was torched. They didn't want us to see these."

Kaylin felt a familiar surge of adrenaline at finally getting a break in their case, till one niggling thought broke through. Who was behind it all?

Hudson returned to his replacement cruiser and opened his laptop. He wanted to do a check on Bart Hardy to see if he had any priors and do a search on the gun. He typed in the van driver's name and waited.

Kaylin sat in the passenger seat and stared out the window.

"What are you thinking?" Hudson now knew that pensive look. She seemed to be in a quandary.

"Just feeling angry they're getting this drug across the border right under our noses. I wonder how many florist vans I've let go by without doing a thorough search." She rubbed her neck muscles. Over and over.

He touched her arm, ignoring the spark igniting between them. Did she feel it, too? He pulled his hand away. Now wasn't the time to think of the beautiful woman beside him. "It's not your fault, Kaylin. They cleverly disguised the plant and would have had the proper certificates, so they sailed across the borders."

"I suppose. Have we heard of anyone overdosing on this drug?"

"No, it doesn't normally kill, but is highly addictive."

She tilted her head and looked at him with an odd expression on her face.

"What?"

"Look at us getting along. I remember how we fought back and forth about Jake's case. Almost to the point of sabotaging everything."

He looked up from his laptop. "I know. I was so self-absorbed back then. I was getting over Rebecca and took my feelings out on you. I was bossy. Can you ever forgive me?"

"I appreciate you saying that. I'm just glad we were able to wrap the case up and book him." She paused. "And of course I forgive you. As they say, it's water under the bridge."

His laptop dinged. He looked down to see a rap sheet appear on his screen, and whistled. "Looks like Bart has been in trouble with the law. Drug arrests, armed robbery and an assault. Seems like the Olivers only hire thugs to bring their flowers across the border. Interesting."

"We need to get a warrant and talk to those owners again. See what's in their back room."

He grabbed the door handle. "Agreed, but for now let's go have a chat with Mr. Hardy."

They stepped out of the cruiser and made their way back into the building.

Kaylin stopped at the vending machine and purchased a snack.

Hudson followed her into the interrogation room. She plunked a water and granola bar on the table in front of the driver. Smart thinking. He was probably hungry from being there for over five hours. The woman knew how to get on his good side.

Bart Hardy grunted. The wiry redheaded twenty-five-year-old slouched in his chair. He chewed his fingernails on one hand and reached for the granola bar with the other.

Why didn't this kid look scared at being detained? Did he care at all? Right now they had him for possessing an unlicensed gun, suspicious pictures that could connect him with the attempted abduction and poppies that could very well be turned into doda. Either he didn't have a clue what he was transporting or he had a good poker face.

Hudson shoved the gun in front of Bart. "This yours?"

The kid's eyes bulged. "Where did that come from?"

"Your glove compartment."

"I didn't put it there. It ain't mine." He opened his water and drank.

Kaylin folded her hands. "You expect us to believe you came all the way across the border and didn't know you were carrying a gun? I find that hard to fathom."

"I'm telling the truth, man. I'm just a driver for DJ's Florist."

Hadn't they heard the same thing from Akio? "How many runs do you make in a month?" Hudson pulled out his notebook. He always took notes the old-fashioned way.

"Two to three. Or sometimes more depending on when the boss wants me to go."

Hudson watched the man's body movements, looking for signs of deceit. "You mean Lyle Oliver?"

"Yes. He and his wife hired me."

"How long have you been working with them?" Kaylin leaned back in her chair.

"Four months now." He unwrapped the granola bar and took a bite.

Hudson tapped his pen on the table. "Do you know Blaine Ridley?"

"Who?"

"Blaine Ridley," Hudson said. "He was a passenger in another DJ's Florist van that was torched."

"I don't know anything about that and I don't know the man." The kid took a drink of water.

Either Bart was a good actor or he clearly didn't know anything. Nothing in his body language showed he was lying. Uninterested, maybe. Hudson decided to try a new tactic. One that should get this kid's attention. "Did you know the last driver that crossed the border was killed by a sniper?"

Bart spat out the water, spraying it over the table. "What? Am I in danger?"

His reaction told Hudson he really didn't know anything. "Tell me about your prior arrests."

"Just some dumb things I did in college. I assure you I'm clean now."

Kaylin tapped the table with her thumb. "What were you supposed to do with the delivery once you brought it across the border?"

"Deliver it to DJ's Florist, of course. What else do you think I'd do with flowers? Sell them on eBay?" He bit into his granola bar.

Hudson was tired of his cocky attitude. "Is that all? What do they do with the dried poppy straw?"

"How do I know? Put it in arrangements, I suspect."

"They never told you anything else about their business?" Hudson stood and leaned against the wall, hooking his thumbs in his belt loops.

"No. Like I said, I only deliver the flowers. Nothing else."

Again, the kid's facial expressions didn't reveal any hidden secrets. Hudson picked up the bag with the pictures and plunked it on the table in front of Bart. "Are these yours?"

"What are they?"

Kaylin removed the pictures from the bag and spread them out. "What does it look like?"

Her cynical words revealed her mood. Seemed she was getting tired of this useless interview.

Hudson, too, was getting annoyed. "We found them taped underneath the passenger seat. You're telling me you didn't know they were there?"

Bart picked up the picture of Kaylin and turned it over. "That's exactly what I'm telling you." He glanced at Kaylin. "This is you."

"Yes, are you targeting me?" Kaylin asked.

"No! I'm innocent. When are you going to let me go? I ain't got nothing more I can tell you." He finished the bar and crumpled up the wrapper. "Should I be calling a lawyer?"

What more could they hold him on? Nothing about his behavior seemed suspicious. They needed to talk to the Olivers and get the scoop on their real business. Clearly there was more going on at DJ's Florist than they let on.

Hudson had one more question for the kid. "You ever hear the name Valentino?"

Bart flinched and looked at his fingers.

Now they were getting somewhere.

Hudson returned to his seat. "Tell me about him."

Bart's face contorted and he rubbed his hands together. "Never met the man."

"But you've heard of him," Hudson said.

"Yes."

Kaylin gathered the pictures and put them back in the bag. "You're in a lot of trouble here. Tell us what you know and perhaps that will help your case." She stood and circled the table.

Bart slumped in his chair. "You have to believe me. I

don't do drugs anymore, but when I was back in college, everyone in the business heard of Valentino."

Why hadn't they? The police had many leads on different drug dealers, so how had Valentino stayed under the radar for so long? Obviously, he was good at hiding. Or had well-placed connections. "Did you deal with him?"

"No one did. He was the big dog and everyone feared him."

"In what way?" Kaylin asked.

"Anyone that tried to skim off the top ended up dead. He has no mercy and he's always watching."

Hudson glanced at Kaylin.

She stopped pacing, eyes widening. Concern crinkled her brow.

Could Valentino be the one targeting her and the chief? If so, why? His need to protect her washed over him again. He would not let anyone hurt her.

Kaylin sat down. "Do you know where we can find him?"

Bart shook his head. "He's everywhere. No one knows."

"How can we get in touch with him?" Hudson tugged at the collar of his gray uniform shirt.

"You don't. He contacts you."

That didn't do them any good. How could they set up a sting without being able to get in touch with him? They needed to find Blaine Ridley. "Do you know anyone else in his organization?"

"He has goons do his dirty work, but I don't know their names." He leaned forward. "Be careful. Word on the street is he's infiltrated the police force."

Hudson's muscles tensed as a thought struck him hard and fast.

Could Valentino be a cop?

Whom could Hudson trust now?

# ELEVEN

Kaylin sat across from Hudson and his boss, Sergeant Peter Miller, at the local police detachment. They'd booked Bart with possession of an unlicensed handgun. They'd confiscated the poppy straw and would be paying the owners of DJ's Florist a visit as soon as they could get a warrant. They had enough evidence against them now to do a thorough search of their premises.

Hudson had also handed over her cell phone to Forensics. They should know soon if the number of whoever sent the text could be traced. She didn't have high hopes. Sergeant Miller passed them copies of the composite sketch of Blaine Ridley. It wasn't much to go on but was all they had.

The excitement of this case fueled her adrenaline and Kaylin's knee bounced in anticipation of the events to come as they planned their next move.

Hudson posted a photo of a dark silhouette on the peg board with the name Valentino beneath it.

Who was this man? Was he part of a local law enforcement agency? Kaylin glanced at Hudson. She knew it couldn't be him. He didn't have an evil bone in his body. Since when had she let go and decided to trust a man? This man?

What about his boss?

The heavyset sergeant in his late fifties looked at the board, his bushy eyebrows knit. He seemed genuinely stumped about the identity of the drug ringleader. "I did a search on Valentino. Nothing came up. Why haven't we heard of him before?"

Hudson shrugged. "Not sure. From what Bart told us, the entire drug gang community is scared of him. Says people would be stupid to cross the man." He groaned. "We need to talk to some dealers. Pressure them. But who?"

Kaylin gasped as someone came to her mind.

She gripped the sides of the table, her knuckles whitening. Past betrayal slammed her in the gut. The thought of having to see the man again turned her stomach, but she knew he might be able to help. She'd set aside her feelings for the sake of the case. She looked up at Hudson. "Jake Shepherd."

Hudson cocked his head. "Are you sure you want to go there again?"

*No, but we have to.*

"He may know something." She turned to Sergeant Miller. "Jake was my fiancé and a drug dealer. He's in the South West Detention Centre."

Peter Miller stood. "I'll call the warden and let them know you're coming. See what you can find out." He left the room.

Hudson grabbed her hand. "I'll be right there with you."

His kind blue eyes stared at her while he caressed the back of her hand with his thumb. His touch soothed the trepidation setting in. She could let him hold her hand all day, but she knew they had a job to do. She pulled away, not letting him see how this simple act had affected her. She stood. "Let's get this over with."

Twenty minutes later, they sat in a small visitation room and waited for Jake to arrive. The guards at the South West Detention Centre had searched them and taken their weapons to be locked up. The vein in her neck pulsed. She needed her gun for comfort. She rarely used it, but knowing she had it when seeing Jake would have set her at ease.

Perspiration formed on her upper lip as spots danced in her vision. She couldn't hyperventilate now, but neither could she forget Jake's last words before the bailiff took him away to jail. "I will get you for this. Just wait and see." She placed her hand on her pulsating heart, willing it to slow down.

She hadn't seen him since that day. In fact, she made a point of sending his letters back. No, Kaylin didn't want to have anything to do with Jake after the heartache he'd caused.

The door opened, leaving her thoughts of past hurts behind. The guard entered with a muscular tattooed man trailing behind. The bald inmate plunked himself in the chair across from them.

"Ja-Jake?" Kaylin stuttered out his name. She had to clamp her mouth shut to keep her jaw from dropping. Gone was the innocent-looking man she remembered. He'd been replaced by a hardened hulk of a human.

He sneered, revealing his crooked teeth. "My love." He reached for her.

She recoiled.

Hudson grabbed Jake's arm and squeezed. "Do that again and I'll have you thrown in solitary."

Jake pulled away, eyes glaring. "Don't touch me, Constable Steeves. I know my rights."

"Calm down. We only want to talk to you." Kaylin took out her notebook. How could she have been attracted to this man? His repulsive look shocked her.

"You with him now?" Jake pointed to Hudson.

"We're working together." She paused. Did she wish for more? No, Hudson would never go for a woman with baggage and she had ample, including the man in front of them.

"What do you want from me? Haven't you created enough problems in my life? If word gets out I'm talking to the cops, I'll have a price on my head."

Like she cared. She kept her thoughts to herself and grabbed a pen from her vest pocket. "Tell us what you know about a man named Valentino."

He jerked back in his chair. "I've only heard of him through other inmates, but he's bad news. Why should I help you?"

Hudson hunched forward, his gaze focusing in on the prisoner. "We might be able to get you more privileges around here."

"Like I want your help, Steeves."

"Come on, Jake. What do you have to lose?" Kaylin would have to appeal to his good side. If he had one.

His jaw twitched. "You don't know Valentino. His clutches run deep. Even in here."

Could this brute of a man be scared of the drug leader? What hold did Valentino have on him? His drug dealings must reach further than they thought. "Anything you can tell us will help."

"Will you visit me?" The prisoner winked.

"That's not negotiable. Answer us or we'll let it leak that you snitched on your fellow inmates," Hudson replied.

Jake flexed his muscles. "I don't know a lot. Just that he's the drug world's bigwig."

"How big?"

"The top. Has gangs across Canada and into Michigan."

Hudson squinted, his disbelief evident. "How come we never heard of him until now?"

"He's kept his identity secret for years," Jake said. "I've

heard he always uses a middle man in his dealings. Never shows his face."

Kaylin shuddered. This man must be good at hiding to have evaded the police radar all these years. "Did you deal with him?"

"No." Jake twiddled his thumbs as if bored of the conversation.

"What type of drugs does Valentino traffic?" Kaylin asked him.

"Heroin, fentanyl. More recently doda. You name it, he's dealt it."

"Have you heard of anyone working for him?" Hudson shifted in his chair.

"Word out on the street is there is a man who deals closely with him."

"Who?" Kaylin held her breath. Would they get a lead?

"Blaine Ridley."

Kaylin glanced at Hudson. Why did this man's name keep coming up?

They had to find him and fast. He could be the key to this doda puzzle.

Hudson holstered his 9 mm after returning from the interrogation with Jake and walked through the prison doors into the heat of the day. He put on his police-issued cap and led Kaylin to his cruiser. Their meeting with Jake solidified the need to find Valentino before he infiltrated the streets with more drugs. His cell phone rang as he opened his car door. He pulled it out of his pocket and glanced at the screen. Peter Miller.

"Hey, Sarge. Just finished with Jake Shepherd." He explained what they'd learned. "We need to find Blaine Ridley. Did we ever get a hit on a hospital check? He was shot at Rossiter's."

"No hits at any hospital or medical center. Must have

gone to a shady doctor or maybe a vet to stay under the radar," Miller said. "I have the entire station hunting him down, and there's a BOLO out on him even though our description isn't the best. He still hasn't returned to his apartment." The sergeant shuffled some papers. "We just got word that Percy Brown was killed from a high dosage of fentanyl."

"Why does that not surprise me?"

"Right, since we're dealing with drug dealers."

"What can I do for you?" His boss always called for a reason. He raised his brow at Kaylin as she got into the vehicle.

"The judge issued your warrant to search DJ's Florist," Miller said.

Finally, a break. He sat in the driver's seat and started the car. "Good. We'll pick it up and head there as soon as we can."

"One more thing. Bianca didn't get any hits on the nurse in the database. Seems like she's a ghost."

"Probably hired by Valentino."

"More than likely. Stay safe."

Hudson pulled the cruiser onto the main road. "That was Miller. No hit on the nurse, but we can pick up the warrant now and head to the florist. I'm anxious to see what's in their back rooms."

She nodded. "Sounds good." She played with the ring on her finger.

"You okay after seeing Jake?"

"A bit unnerved." She paused. "He sure has changed and not for the good. Looks hardened."

"Guess that's what prison life does to you." He passed a truck on the busy freeway. Traffic picked up in the noon rush. He weaved in and out of the lanes, making his way back to the station.

Twenty minutes later, he parked in front of Miller's car.

"This should only take a minute. Let's see if they found out anything about your cell phone."

His boss met them at the door, shoving the warrant in his hands. "Get down there and see what you can find out. But first, we just had an anonymous tip of a man matching Ridley's description spotted among our homeless. Check it out before you go to DJ's." He stormed back into his office.

"Well, he's Mr. Grumpy Pants." Kaylin chuckled.

"What else is new?" Hudson guided her toward the forensics area and stopped at Bianca's table. "Hey, Bianca. Any word on Kaylin's cell phone? Were you able to trace the texts?"

"Well, hello to you, too, Constable." She held up a bag with the cell phone in it. "Just got the results. They were extremely fast because nothing came up. Burner phone. Sorry."

Kaylin frowned. "Figures. Why am I not surprised?"

"Happens all the time." Bianca picked up another cell phone and handed it to her. "We want you to have this police-issued phone. They won't get this number."

Kaylin put it in her pocket. "Let's hope so. Whoever *they* are, they're always one step ahead of us."

"Right." Bianca held up a file and turned to Hudson. "Ident examined the powder you got from Benji's locker. It's definitely refined poppy straw."

Hudson opened the folder. "We found dried poppy straw in the van the border patrol intercepted. It has to be the way they're getting the drug into the country."

"But why not harvest their own poppy fields? It doesn't make sense. Why take the chance at the border?" Kaylin leaned against the table.

"Good question. Maybe it's easier than planting it

themselves. More convenient." Bianca took a sip of her coffee.

"Whatever the reason, we need to find where they're refining it and fast." Hudson handed her back the file. "Thanks again, Bianca."

Right now it was time to check out the anonymous tip. Maybe they would find Blaine hiding with the homeless. It was the perfect place to blend in. Hudson knew his way around that crowd, so hopefully they'd have a much-needed advantage.

Fifteen minutes later, he parked along the road where he knew most of the homeless lived. "Let's start here."

Cardboard boxes lined the area. Makeshift homes littered the small park across the street with shopping carts outside each one. A bonfire burned in a steel drum despite the heat of the day. Logs crackled as the sparks spat out the top. Local authorities tried to get these men and women to leave, but they didn't have any success. They kept coming back, so the cops gave up after a while. Different missions visited the area to hand out blankets and food.

Hudson knew because he'd been helping out since he was a teenager. Both on the streets and at the local homeless shelter. It was where he'd met his friend Layke Jackson.

A gray-haired woman peeked out from her tattered blanket and smiled a toothless grin. Hudson stopped at her feet. "Mary, good to see you. How are you?"

Mary was a favorite and got along with practically everyone. Not like some of the homeless who fought over territories.

"I'm surviving among these animals." She got up and pointed to a man poking his head into a nearby garbage bin. She turned to Kaylin. "My dear. It's been forever since I've seen you. Where have you been keeping yourself?"

Hudson raised a brow. Mary knew Kaylin? How?

Kaylin gave the older woman a hug. "I'm surprised you remember me after all these years."

"Mary doesn't forget a face, love. Especially one of her own."

*Wait—what? One of her own?*

What did that mean?

Kaylin kept her gaze on the woman and pulled out the sketch of Blaine. "Perhaps you can help us. Have you seen this man?"

Mary leaned in, her mouth forming an O.

"Why, yes. Hard to forget that scar. I saw him yesterday. Tried to steal food from me. Told him that no one steals from Mary. She gives it away. Gave him a slice of bread."

"Then what happened?" Hudson let go of his questions for Kaylin, but he certainly would inquire later.

"Nothing. He just limped away," Mary said.

*Limped.* That had to be Blaine; he'd been shot in the leg. Hudson shifted his weight. "What time was this?"

Mary tapped her dimpled chin. "Nine thirty p.m. I remember because I was about to turn in for the night when I saw the time on the digital sign at the gas station across the street."

"Have you seen him since?" Kaylin took the sketch back.

"Nope."

"Can you tell us anything about him? Was he nervous? Did he seem angry?" Hudson gazed around the area, taking it all in.

"Now that you mention it, he kept checking his phone and looking behind him like he was scared someone was following him." She pulled a toothpick from her pocket and stuck it in her mouth.

"Anything else?"

"You can check at the shelter. Saw him heading in that direction." She crawled back into her tent.

"Let's talk with some of the others." Kaylin walked on to another home, bent down and shook the older man's hand.

Over the next hour, they scoured the area looking for clues of Blaine's whereabouts. Other vagrants claimed to have seen him but only yesterday. How could he have disappeared so quickly, especially since he was wounded?

"Let's head to the shelter and ask there. Maybe he stopped in for lunch or dinner." Hudson removed his hat and wiped the sweat from his forehead.

They patrolled down the road and stepped into the establishment funded by local churches. The bells on the door announced their presence. A waft of baking bread greeted them. Hudson's mouth watered.

"Hudson!" Kurt, the head of the shelter, rushed to meet them. "So good to see you again. Missed you last week."

"I wasn't able to join my church in helping serve. Working on a case." He gestured toward Kaylin. "Kurt, this is—"

"Kaylin! I almost didn't recognize you in your uniform." He pulled her into a hug. "When was the last time you visited us?"

Hudson's jaw dropped as he looked at her. Here, too? What other surprises was Kaylin holding back?

She avoided Hudson's gaze. "Too long, Kurt. How are you?"

"I'm good. I see by your uniform you're now with CBSA. So glad you overcame your situation."

She cleared her throat and pulled out Blaine's sketch. "Maybe you can help us. Have you seen this man?"

It was obvious to Hudson that Kaylin didn't want to talk about her past. She was holding out on him. When had she frequented this place?

Kurt studied the composite. "Yes. He came here last night as I was closing, demanding food and money."

"What did you do?" Hudson took out his notebook and jotted down some notes, creating a timeline. 9:30 p.m. left Mary. 9:45 p.m. stopped by the shelter.

"Told him we don't keep cash here, but I could scrounge up some food," Kurt said. "He waited until I made him a goody bag."

"How did he seem?" Kaylin tucked the picture back in her vest pocket. "Agitated? Nervous?"

"Both. Kept looking out the door as if someone was following him. I asked him if he needed help in finding a place to stay, but he grabbed the food and hobbled out the door. Didn't come back today."

Was Ridley strapped for cash? Was he trying to stay under the wire from the drug ring?

Hudson handed Kurt a card. "Can you give me a call if he returns?"

"Sure thing. See you next week?"

"If I can get this case wrapped up. Take care, Kurt." Hudson put his hat back on.

"Will do. Nice seeing you, Kaylin."

"You, too."

Hudson held the door open for her and they stepped out onto the sidewalk. "Tell me, when were you here and how do you know Mary?"

Her facial expression clouded before she looked away.

He grabbed her hand. "You can tell me, Kaylin. I won't tell anyone."

She shook her head. "That part of my life is over and none of your concern."

Her sharp tone stopped him in his tracks. "I'm sorry. I didn't mean to intrude. You can talk to me anytime."

"Nothing to say, Hudson." She continued walking.

He rushed to catch up. "Fine, I'll—"

His cell phone buzzed. He hit the answer button without looking at the caller. "Steeves here."

"Get to DJ's Florist shop." Miller's booming voice commanded obedience.

Hudson perked up. "Heading there now. What's going on?"

"It's on fire."

Hudson studied the wreckage at DJ's Florist. Blackened beams from the building's structure were the only thing left standing. The firefighters couldn't save it. The owner and his wife had been inside and suffered smoke inhalation. They had been whisked off to the hospital. The fire chief and the inspector shuffled through what used to be the flower shop's showroom. Even from a distance, smoke filled Hudson's nose and he sneezed. Chief Harrison almost didn't let them stay in the area but the warrant and his explanation of why they needed to check for evidence convinced him. The chief would look for them, but they were not allowed to enter the premises.

Chief Harrison used a pole to sift through the ashes. He turned and yelled to them. "What are you looking for?"

"Anything that can tie the Olivers to a drug smuggling ring. We wanted to get into their back rooms, but now you can't even tell the showroom from their offices." Hudson changed his stance, clasping his hands behind him.

The chief pointed. "Looks like this frame could be the entrance of a new room."

Kaylin sneezed. "This pungent smell is overwhelming." She pointed to the wreckage. "Everything is gone."

"O ye of little faith," Hudson said. "I'm praying God will help us find something."

She wrinkled her nose.

Did she know how cute she was when she made that face?

*Hudson, quit staring.* He studied his feet. He tried to stop his growing feelings for her, but to no avail. He enjoyed her company. Once this case was wrapped up, would she want to be a friend? But did he want more?

At least that was what his heart told him.

His head told him she wasn't a believer. It would never work.

He kicked a stone, sending it across the sidewalk. "Don't you believe in prayer?"

"Nope. Never did me any good."

"What do you mean? When did God supposedly fail you?"

She rolled her eyes. "You mean how many times?"

"Tell me about it."

"It's in the past and forgotten." She focused back on the chief and the inspector rummaging through the ashes.

There was no way she'd put whatever happened to her behind her. It was still written on her face. Hudson could see that she needed forgiveness in her life.

*But have you forgiven yourself?*

The thought raced through his mind before he could stop it. Could he put his past behind him, too?

Kaylin's hand flew to her chest. "This can't be a coincidence."

"What do you mean?" Hudson rubbed his sinuses, pulling himself out of his thoughts about her.

"The shop is on fire just after we pick up the warrant to search the place? Someone knew we were coming."

Hudson nodded. "Agreed."

Chief Harrison rushed toward them, raising a steel box. "We found something hidden in what was left of one wall."

Hudson put on his gloves and took the box from the chief. He set it on his cruiser and wiped the ashes from the top. A charred lock held it shut. "Whatever is in here was important enough to keep secret. Do you have bolt cutters in your rig?"

The chief yelled to a firefighter to bring the tools. Seconds later, a stocky fireman handed them to Hudson.

Hudson broke the lock and lifted the lid. It creaked open. A ledger lay tucked inside. The steel box had kept it untouched from the raging flames.

Perhaps it was the evidence they waited for.

Kaylin leaned over his shoulder as he opened the book. A key fell out.

Hudson picked it up. "I wonder what this is to." He put it back in the box and focused on the journal. "Looks like dates and times of some sort of exchange." Hudson skimmed down the entries with his index finger and stopped on a name.

Blaine Ridley.

"There's that name again." Kaylin pointed to another name. Valentino. "It says shipment to Blaine. Could this be their ledger passing over the poppy straw?"

"Looks like it. We need—"

His cell phone chimed with a text message from his boss.

Ident found traces of another drug in Matthew's blood, but they're still analyzing it. Plus, the angle of the injection is wrong since he's left-handed. Now treating this as attempted murder.

Hudson slumped against his cruiser and rubbed the back of his neck. *Lord, help me to solve this case before other teens are targeted.*

# TWELVE

Kaylin turned the pages of the ledger at the police interrogation room and studied the entries, trying to make sense of it all. After a few minutes she slammed the book shut and shoved it across the table. The documentation confused her. The dates and times of the drug meets didn't add up. She and Hudson had left the fire scene and it was now well after the dinner hour. Her stomach growled, reminding her she hadn't eaten all day. She'd require some food soon or her weary body would cave.

As if he'd heard her thoughts, Hudson entered with subs and set one in front of her. His clouded eyes revealed his concern over the news of his nephew's attempted murder. Who would want to kill the teen? Had he gotten too close to drug dealers? If so, which ones?

Her mouth watered as she took a bite of the turkey club. She let the delicious taste linger a second before swallowing. It was just what she needed. She opened up the ledger and pointed to some entries. "Look how they've recorded a shipment arriving on one day and out the next week. Perhaps they held the poppy straw before handing it off to the buyer. But why? You would think they'd want to get it out of their shop right away."

"Could they be drying it more to get it ready for refining?"

She pinched her lips together. "I wish we could talk to the Olivers. Find out more about it and these entries."

"The head nurse at the hospital told me tomorrow

morning would be best." Hudson took a bite of his sub and swallowed. "I want to know more about the fire. Was it arson?" He picked up the evidence bag containing the key. "This has to be valuable because why else would they lock it in a box?"

"Agreed, but there's no way to know what it unlocks. There's no engraving on it."

"More dead ends," Hudson said.

"Did you believe Bart when he said Valentino infiltrated the police force? Maybe someone in your office?"

Hudson slumped back in his chair. "I hope not."

"But how else did Blaine or Valentino know we had a warrant and were headed to DJ's? It's the only thing that makes sense."

He let out a heavy sigh. "I can't imagine anyone on my team being bought by a drug kingpin."

Kaylin rubbed her chin. "But how well do we really know people?" Her dad was good at playing the game. A sweetheart at church, but a monster behind closed doors.

"True." Hudson's cell phone rang. "Steeves here." He paused. "Chief Harrison, I'll put you on speaker phone."

He set the phone on the table between them. "Go ahead."

"We know what caused the fire at DJ's Florist," the chief said.

Kaylin leaned forward, her chin resting on her hand. She waited with bated breath at the news. "What?"

"Arson. We found a gas can in the alley behind the shop. Seems pretty stupid to leave the evidence behind."

Hudson sipped his soda. "Obviously, whoever started the fire didn't care if we found out it was arson. Pretty blatant."

"Can we check the can for fingerprints?" Kaylin wrote "Arson but by who?" in her notebook.

"Send it to Bianca, Chief," Hudson said. "If there are fingerprints on it, the Ident team will find them."

"Will do. Chat later." He clicked off the call.

"Doesn't surprise me." Kaylin took the final bite of her sub and crumpled up the wrapper.

Hudson leafed through the ledger. "This book is full of entries. Looks like this arrangement has been going on for a couple of years."

"But I thought doda was just making a comeback."

"It is, but we had takedowns as far back as nine years ago. It died down, but for some reason it has become the drug of choice lately."

"What makes it so special?"

"Perhaps because it's easier to traffic under the radar."

They spent the next couple of hours poring over the entries, looking for a common thread. Each delivery had the same MO. Shipment arrived one day and left one week later.

She glanced at her watch. Nine thirty. "Anything else to investigate tonight?"

"I think we've had enough for one day. How about we meet early tomorrow? Say seven?" He threw his sub wrapper in the nearby trash can.

She gathered her belongings and stood. "Okay, then. I'm headed back to Diane's. See you tomorrow."

He rubbed her arm. "Stay safe."

His tender touch soothed her. The handsome officer certainly knew how to draw a woman in. His smile illuminated his face. She studied his lips and imagined them on hers. Would they be soft? Smooth?

*Stop it, Kaylin. He's off-limits. So are you. Remember the baggage.*

She shifted her weight in order to change her concentration and stop the romantic thoughts. "Will do."

Kaylin exited into the parking lot.

The night air's mugginess washed over her tired body. She removed the elastic from her ponytail and fluffed her hair, letting the gentle breeze flow through it. The day had been full of adventure but also dead ends. Hopefully tomorrow would be better and the interview with the Olivers informative. They needed answers.

Fifteen minutes later, she opened the door at Diane's darkened house. Had she gone to bed early? Kaylin flipped the kitchen light on and stopped in her tracks.

Dishes lay broken on the floor. The table was over-turned, chairs smashed.

A sob caught in her throat. "Diane?"

A squeak on the wooden floor to the right caught her attention. She turned, but too late.

A wet cloth was clamped over her mouth and leathery hands grabbed her into a vise grip. She struggled to free herself, till the scent of chloroform reached her nostrils.

Darkness entangled her, pulling her into its deadly clutches.

Kaylin bolted awake, gasping for air from a dream that was more like a nightmare. Her heart thumped as she looked around the room. She lay on a wooden bench; restraints bound her hands and ankles. Where was she? How long had she been out? She checked her watch. 7:30 a.m. She'd been unconscious all night. Had Hudson started a search for her when she didn't show up at their meeting that morning?

Mustiness filled her nose. The room's dampness sent shivers racing through her body. She looked around and saw a canoe on the other side of the room. Lawn chairs were piled up beside it. Waves crashed outside the small building. Someone had brought her to a boathouse. But who was her captor?

She pulled at the ropes on her wrists. If she could only

free herself, she could untie her feet and escape before who-ever held her returned. She bit the restraints and tugged.

Her breath came in rapid bursts. She threw her hands back in her lap as tears stung her eyes. It was useless. The ropes were too tight.

Had someone left her here to die?

Surely God had abandoned her?

Again.

She could almost hear Diane tell her to trust God and that He would never leave her.

Diane. Was she okay?

Her muscles tightened as fear and panic threatened to overtake her. Before she realized what she said, she heard herself pray. "God? Are You there?" Heat flushed her cheeks. "I can't find You. Please show me where to look."

Tears flowed down her cheeks as Diane's face flashed before her. God had given her this amazing woman who'd taken her in when she'd felt abandoned by her father. Where would she have been without her? Still on the streets with those vagrants who'd tried to attack her.

Maybe God had watched over her, but she had failed to see it. She hung her head. How could she have been so blind?

"I'm sorry, God. Can You forgive me?"

She jerked her head up. If she wanted God to forgive her, she'd also have to do the same with her father. Impos-sible. She couldn't. Did that make her a terrible person? Unlovable? No one had cared for her as a child, and when she grew up, even Jake had failed to love her. Except for when it had suited him.

Her brother had abandoned her, too.

No one loved her.

Wait. Diane had told her God loved her uncondition-ally. It didn't matter what she had done in her life, He would always be there for her. No matter what. He had paid the ultimate price for her. All she'd learned at church came tumbling back like a snowball rolling downhill, collecting snow and growing. It overwhelmed her, causing her heart to tighten.

She sobbed. Was it true? Could it be that He had never left her? That she had been the one who had moved away?

Kaylin wiped her tears with the back of her bound hands. "God, if You're there, save me. I surrender myself to You."

Peace washed over her like a bucket of cold water dumped on her during a warm summer day. She breathed in and exhaled loudly. *God's got this.* She heard the words Diane always said to her.

Now she finally believed it.

"Thank You, God." A smile tugged at her lips before forming. He now lived in her.

Footsteps sounded outside the boathouse, wrenching her from her thoughts.

Her heartbeat caught in her throat, holding her captive.

The door creaked open and her captor stepped into the sun's rays shining through the window. His face no longer featureless.

She fought for a breath.

Jake?

Hudson checked his watch for the fifth time. 7:45 a.m. Where was Kaylin? He tightened his jaw. He grabbed his cell phone and punched in her new number, tapping his toe as he waited. All he got was voice mail. Again.

"Ugh!" He threw the cell phone on his desk.

"What's up, Steeves?"

Hudson jumped, knocking over his pens, and turned around to see his boss. "Don't sneak up on me like that."

"Why are you so grumpy?"

He shook his head. He had to rein in his feelings and fast. He bent over and gathered his pens, putting them back in the holder. "Kaylin was supposed to be here at seven. We wanted to run to the hospital early to interrogate the Olivers."

"Call her again. We don't have time to wait around." He stormed back into his office.

The vein in Hudson's neck pulsed. Ever since his witness had died in that previous case, his boss had had it in for him. What did he have to do to prove his worth?

He grabbed his phone and tried Kaylin again. Voice mail. It wasn't like her to be late. He dialed Diane's number. No answer. What was going on?

His cell phone rang. "Steeves here."

"Constable Steeves, this is Brett Walker. I'm the warden at the South West Detention Centre."

Hudson perked up. "How can I help you?"

"You left your card with one of the guards to advise you if anything of interest came up on the prisoner Jake Shepherd. I wanted to let you know he escaped our custody last night."

"What?" Hudson sprang out of his chair. "Why am I only being informed now?"

"The guard who had your card just came on duty."

"What happened?"

"We were transferring him to the maximum security site of Collins Bay Institution in Kingston. The van was in an accident and he got loose. We haven't been able to locate him."

The hair on his arms prickled. Kaylin's absence and Jake's escape couldn't be a coincidence. Something wasn't right.

*Lord, help me to be wrong. Protect her.*

"I appreciate you letting me know. Keep me updated."

"Will do."

Hudson clicked off the call and ran into his boss's office. "Jake Shepherd escaped custody last night and Kaylin is missing. This isn't good."

Miller whistled. "Take a drive to her place. See if she's there. We'll try and triangulate her cell."

"I'm guessing it's off because it keeps going to voice mail right away. I'll check her friend Diane's place, where she's been staying, and get back to you." He rushed out to his cruiser and squealed out of the parking lot, turning on his siren and flashing lights. He needed to make it to Diane's place as fast as he could.

Seven minutes later, he pulled in front of Diane's house and jumped out of the vehicle.

Kaylin's Honda was not parked in the driveway. Her protection detail was missing. *Someone will pay for this.*

He took the front steps two at a time and stopped. The door was ajar. He pulled out his 9 mm and stepped through the entrance. "Kaylin? Diane? Are you here?"

Moans sounded upstairs.

He inched his way up, hugging the wall while raising his weapon. "Kaylin? Diane?"

More muffled screams.

He opened the bedroom door to find an older woman on the bed, gagged and tied to the headboard.

He holstered his gun and ran to her side. He pulled the gag off and untied her. "Where's Kaylin?" He didn't recognize his own shaky voice. *Get a grip. You're not helping anyone by panicking.*

"I don't know, but a masked man broke into my house and tied me up. I heard Kaylin come home, but then nothing." Her hair was matted to her head, her eyes wild.

Kaylin was gone.

Jake had taken her. It was the only answer.

*I have to find Kaylin, Lord. Before he hurts her.*

Hudson had seen the look in Jake's eyes when he'd spoken to Kaylin at the detention center. He was still infatuated with her, and the fact that she'd helped put him away must have only escalated his anger.

She was in immediate danger.

He looked down at the woman who he knew had to be Diane. "You okay? Did he hurt you?"

"No." Tears welled in her eyes. "Find Kaylin."

He pulled out his phone and hit Sergeant Miller's number. "Anything, Steeves?"

"She's not here and her car is gone. What about her cell phone?"

"It's off. I've put out a BOLO for her car and have contacted the OPP and Windsor police to help scour the city. Even CBSA officers are hunting. We'll find her."

He gripped his cell phone tighter. "Why wasn't an officer watching her?"

"I pulled them."

"You what?"

Why would his boss pull the Windsor police chief's daughter's protection? Something was not right.

"You heard me. We need to cut down on overtime costs. I had to do it."

There had to be more to the story, but Hudson put it behind him. He had to concentrate on Kaylin right now. "Listen, send Forensics to this address." He gave the sergeant Diane's address and filled him in on the situation he'd found at the scene. "She's okay, but we need Forensics to check her place out." He tugged at his collar. "Jake Shepherd is dangerous. Do a full sweep on him. Places he visited, properties he owned. All of it."

"I'll get Ident out there right away and have Bianca investigate Shepherd."

Hudson shoved his cell phone into his pocket. He needed to find Kaylin. But where should he start?

*Think, Hudson, think.*

Before it was too late.

# THIRTEEN

Kaylin stared into the ruthless eyes of Jake Shepherd. The hulk stood over her smiling. He ran his fingers down her arm and she cringed, wiggling in her restraints. Even if she could get free, there was no way she'd be able to take this muscular man down. She'd have to outsmart him instead. But how?

"I've been waiting for this day." He circled the bench, stopping to caress her arms and face. "I've missed you." His raspy voice personified evil.

Her body quivered. Was this really happening? "How did you get out of jail, Jake?"

"Does it matter? I'm free and we can be together now."

Her muscles flinched. "That will never happen."

He leaned down, so he was inches away from her face. "Why? You don't think Hudson is going to come to your rescue, do you?"

His coffee breath repulsed her and she turned her head to stop the nausea. "He'll find you."

His laughter boomed in the small boathouse. "He doesn't even know you're missing. I drove us here in your car."

No! It can't be.

*God, help me. Show me what to do.*

He grabbed her cheeks and turned her head back to look at him. "You put me away, and I always said I'd get even with you. You'll do as I say or face the consequences."

He slapped her.

Her cheek stung at his attack and tears threatened to fall. She inhaled a rattled breath, holding it for five seconds. She wouldn't give him the satisfaction of seeing her cry. She turned her head. That was when she spotted it. Her cell phone sat on a ledge beside the door. She needed to get to it.

"Do you know what I went through in prison? Beatings upon beatings until I finally worked up my strength to get back at the gangs in there. They never knew what hit them. Even killed a man."

He was a murderer, too? There was no telling what he'd do to her if she didn't give in to his demands.

*I'm going to die. Just as I was getting to know You, Lord.*

Her palms turned clammy. What could she do? She wiggled her hands to see if she could slip them out. This time she felt the restraints loosen. She had to keep him talking. Give Hudson time to find her. "Why did you get into selling drugs, Jake? You had it all. Good job. Me. What happened?" She twisted her hands again.

"It wasn't enough. I wanted more. More money, more prestige."

"But don't you know money isn't everything?"

He walked to the small window and peered out. "Oh yes, it is, and I'm going to make a fortune."

What did he mean? He should have learned his lesson the first time. Obviously, jail time hadn't made him any smarter. "And how do you plan on doing that?"

"I have my ways and they involve you."

She grimaced. "I will not help you do anything. You hear me?"

"Yes, you will."

"Hudson will stop you."

He grunted. "Hardly. I'm going to keep you away from him. Now he'll have to pay the price."

She needed to stop him from hurting Hudson. Images of what he'd do to the handsome constable exploded through her mind, leaving her breathless. "Keep him out of it. We're just working on a case together. That's all."

Even though she wished they were more.

The realization startled her. When had her feelings for Hudson changed? They'd only started working together a few days ago.

"Liar. I can see it in your eyes. You like him," Jake spat out. "Didn't you get my text? I warned you, but you didn't listen."

He was behind the texts? What about the intruder in her home? Had that been his doing, too? "How did you get a phone to text me? And how did you get my number?"

"I bribed a guard and he got me a burner. Hid it in a hole in the wall." He smirked. "A black hat hacker got me your number."

"Who ransacked my apartment?" She pulled at the ropes. They loosened more.

He rubbed his bald head. "I had an ex-con do that for me. He kept me informed of your shenanigans. How you've been hanging around Steeves. Even after my warning, you still didn't listen."

"Tell me about your plan to make money." As much as it chilled her to hear his plans for her, she had to keep him talking.

"You'll see." His cell phone rang and he turned his back toward her. "Yup. Got what you want. Where can we meet?"

Who was he talking to?

"Got it. See you then." He walked over and grabbed her by the arm. "Get up. We're going for a walk."

"How can I with ropes around my ankles?" One more wiggle and she would be free of her hand restraints.

He untied her feet and pulled her up.

The ropes on her hands loosened enough for her to shimmy out of them.

She mustered up courage and thrust her elbow deep into his stomach with all her strength.

He doubled over and lost his balance.

She rushed over to the ledge, snatched her cell phone and raced out of the boathouse.

Hudson's cell phone buzzed. He grabbed it out of his pocket and swiped the screen. Kaylin.

*Thank You, Lord.*

"Kaylin, where are you?" He sat up straighter in his car and pressed the cell phone harder into his ear to hear her every word.

"At a boathouse somewhere by the river." Her words came out breathless.

She was running.

"Is Jake with you?"

"I escaped, but he's on my tail." A horn sounded in the distance through the phone.

"Can you see where you are? Any landmarks?" He started his cruiser and pulled out of Diane's driveway.

"I can see the Windsor Harbor. I'm east of it."

He did a U-turn, flipped on his siren and headed in that direction.

"I'm coming. See anything else?" He passed cars, driving in the left lane on the freeway.

"There's a—"

A crash sounded through the phone, followed by silence.

"Kaylin? Are you there? Kaylin, talk to me."

"She's mine now, Steeves." Jake's gruff voice rumbled through the phone.

*Click.*

Hudson's heart thumped. He had to get to her and fast. He pressed the accelerator and punched in Bianca's number.

"How can I help you, Constable?"

He explained where Kaylin was located. "Did you happen to find a boathouse owned by Jake?"

He could hear her as she clicked on her keyboard. "Yes, his family owned one. Here's the address."

Hudson memorized it. "Thanks, Bianca. Tell the Sarge where I'm headed. Get the cavalry here."

"If I can find him. He left earlier and was all mysterious about where he was going."

The hairs on his neck stung, sending him on high alert. What was his boss up to? "He probably had an appointment."

"Could be, but why not say so? Anyway, go get Kaylin."

He disconnected and threw his cell phone on the seat, taking a sharp right toward the marina. The boathouse wasn't far from there. *Lord, help me not to be too late.*

Hudson slowed as he came in view of a row of houses situated close to the pier. Boathouses lined the river's edge. He checked the numbers and stopped in front of the one Bianca gave him. He jumped out of the cruiser and unleashed his 9 mm. He couldn't wait for backup. Kaylin was in danger. He dashed to the backyard, taking shelter behind trees as he dodged between them.

Loud voices sounded from the other side of the boathouse.

He crept closer, crouching low.

"You got away from me once, but I have you now."

Jake's creepy voice sounded above the waves lapping against the pier.

Hudson edged his way around the building.

Jake had his gun pressed in Kaylin's temple and held her by her waist. They stood on the dock, close to a boat anchored to the side.

"Hudson's on his way, Jake," he heard Kaylin say. "You lose."

Her captor's eyes narrowed. "He can't have you. You're mine."

Hudson couldn't take a shot without risking Kaylin's life. He had no choice but to talk him down. Hudson stepped into view, his gun in front of him. "Jake, it's over. Let her go."

Jake pulled Kaylin tighter. "I'll shoot her."

"Give it up, man." He stepped closer. He had to get her away from this man.

"Stay back," Jake said.

Sirens screamed nearby. The cavalry was coming.

Jake pushed her closer to the water's edge.

*No, not water.*

A tremor snaked up his spine. His hands turned clammy and his gun slipped. His fear of water resurfaced. He took a step back. Images flashed of him as a young boy flailing in the ocean as a wave slammed him to the bottom while his breath evaporated. He closed his eyes to push the scene away. For Kaylin's sake.

*Give me strength, Lord.*

He opened his eyes and stepped toward the pier.

The sirens grew louder.

Dread surged through his body and he gripped his gun tighter, raising it higher. "You're out of time, Jake. Let. Her. Go."

"She belongs to me and now to someone else. The exchange will happen. Her life for my fortune."

"What are you talking about?"

Kaylin's lips trembled. "I thought you loved me, Jake."

"You betrayed me." He pointed the gun in Hudson's direction. "For him. Besides, I'm going to be rich."

"Who are you talking about?" Hudson split his stance and kept his gun trained on the bulky man. A million scenarios to save Kaylin raced through his mind, but he stood still. He would not put her life in jeopardy.

"There's a contract out for her life on the dark web. Million dollars for her. Alive."

What? Hudson had to contain this situation. Could this have anything to do with her attempted abductions? "Tell me more."

"They promised money if I brought her to him."

That didn't make any sense. "Who?"

"That's their secret." He curved his lips upward.

Hudson moved forward slightly. "Give me their contact information. Do you know who they are?"

Jake looked from Hudson to Kaylin, inching her closer to the end of the pier. "Why would I—"

A shot boomed.

Jake stumbled into Kaylin. She lost her balance and plummeted into the water, whacking her head on the side.

Jake lay in a pool of blood, his hand dangling over the edge.

"No!" Hudson ran down the pier and looked into the water.

Kaylin sank into the murky river, with her face submerged.

*Lord, no!*

He hesitated.

Images of the witness he watched drown floated into

his consciousness. He couldn't let that happen again. Especially with Kaylin's life at risk.

*You can do this.*

He took a breath and plunged into the water.

Hudson exploded to the surface, drew in air and dove deeper toward Kaylin. He tugged on her arm and pulled her up, ensuring her head was above the water. Her motionless body bobbed up and down. He had to get her to the shore and perform CPR.

He towed Kaylin beside him as he swam through the cold, cloudy water. His shoes threatened to pull him down, but he kept kicking. The shore was in sight. Just a few more strokes. He lost his grip and began to sink, his limbs like jelly. His strength wavered and he sent up a prayer.

*God, give me strength.*

He grabbed Kaylin under her arms and swam as fast as he could. Reaching the shore, he pulled her to the beach and turned her over. He pumped her chest and performed CPR.

She didn't respond.

"Kaylin, come back to me." He breathed into her mouth once again, her lips cold. He couldn't lose her. Feelings swept over him and they couldn't be squelched.

He pumped her chest again.

Policemen made their way down the beach. An ambulance arrived seconds later. The paramedics jumped from their vehicle and raced toward them.

Kaylin still lay motionless.

He breathed into her mouth again.

*Please, God. Save her.*

She coughed and water spewed from her mouth.

He turned her to her side as more water gushed out.

"Thank God, you're okay." Hudson peered into her eyes. "I almost lost you."

She wrapped her arms around his neck and cried. "Thank you."

He hugged her tighter. "You're safe now."

"Jake…?"

"He's dead."

She pulled back and rubbed her head. "That's gonna hurt worse later. Did you catch the shooter?"

"I was too busy saving you." He'd brief the Windsor police and get them to scour the area to find where the shot came from. He guessed the shooter was long gone. He'd taken down his target and fled.

He pushed wet hair off her face and caressed her cheek. "I panicked when I couldn't find you, Kaylin," he admitted. He looked into her eyes and was overcome with feelings for this woman.

When a tear rolled down her cheek, he wiped it away with his thumb. "Did he do anything to you?" The thought of Jake hurting her, stalking her, set his heart on edge. He drew in a jagged breath.

"No. God saved me."

He exhaled. Wait. She'd admitted God had helped her. "What do you mean, Kaylin?"

"I found God in that boathouse. I sensed His hand on me and I surrendered."

*Thank You, Lord.*

He pulled her closer. "I'm glad."

Could they be together now?

He squeezed his eyes shut like his heart. No, he couldn't fall again even though he knew his heart was past the point of no return. He had to let her go. She deserved someone who could love her.

He released her. "Tell me what happened."

Kaylin briefed him on how Jake had abducted her, how she'd woken up bound in the boathouse and how he'd taunted her. She'd escaped thanks to God. That was how she put it.

"God protected you." Hudson's cell phone rang but he ignored it.

"I know, and I saw how He's kept me from harm all my life, but I refused to see it." Her eyes widened. "Is Diane okay? Her house was trashed."

He nodded. "She's fine, only rattled. Forensics is scouring her place as we speak. What do you—"

"Step aside, Officer." A stocky paramedic came up and knelt beside them. "We need to examine the patient."

Hudson stood. "Take care of her."

He walked away to let them do their work. For the next ten minutes they examined her and asked questions. They suggested she go to the hospital but she refused, insisting she felt fine. Just a little shaken.

Hudson reveled in her stamina and in the news of her conversion. What did she mean that God had kept her safe all her life? He wanted to find out.

Hudson briefed the officers on the scene and suggested they check out the area for places where the shooter could have positioned himself. They dispersed in different directions.

The coroner arrived and examined Jake's body. He'd been taken down by a clean shot to the temple. Assassin style. Like Akio Lee, Hudson recalled. Obviously someone didn't want Jake to talk. Who?

As the coroner's office took Jake away, Hudson's cell phone buzzed again.

His boss. He was back from wherever he'd gone. "Hey, Sarge. We found her and she's okay." He briefed him on the situation and Jake's death.

"Glad to hear you got to her in time. Who knows what he may have done. We'll put Bianca on checking the dark web."

Hudson cringed at the thought of what she would find. "Good. What's up?"

"Bad news. We just learned two teenagers died of a doda overdose."

He tightened his grip on his phone. "What? That doesn't happen with doda."

"It has. A forensic pathologist is doing the autopsy and will do a full tox screen to see what we're dealing with. We're waiting on Matthew's test, too."

He bristled. "Let me know if anything comes up."

"Oh, and Hudson, Benji Rossiter was also found at the house where the teenagers died."

Hudson ran his fingers through his wet buzz-cut hair. "Was he one of the victims?"

"No, but he's in a coma. Head to the hospital."

He gritted his teeth. "Will do. I'll keep you informed."

Kaylin raised her eyebrow. "What's going on?"

He hesitated. Could she deal with this now after what she'd been through?

She stood. "Come on, tell me. I'm okay."

"Benji is in a coma." He explained what Miller had told him.

She wiped the sand from her uniform. "Let's get going, then. We need to see him."

"Shouldn't you sit this one out? Get some rest. You've been through quite an ordeal."

She shook her head. "Not a chance. Just swing by my apartment so I can change."

"Fine. We'll get someone to check your car for evidence before releasing it back to you."

"Let's go."

Fifty minutes later, after they were both able to change out of their wet clothes, they arrived at Windsor Regional Hospital to check on Benji. They walked down the corridor and into his room.

Benji lay motionless, with a breathing apparatus hooked up to him. His heart monitor beeped a steady rhythm.

Poor kid. Just couldn't shake the drugs.

David Rossiter stood at their interruption and threw his work folder on the bed. "What are you doing here?"

"We heard about Benji," Hudson said. "How is he?"

"Fighting for his life. What do you think?"

Kaylin sat beside the bed and took Benji's hand. "We're praying for him."

David grunted. "Like that will help."

"I used to think that, too, but God recently showed me He's here. We just need to trust." Kaylin's words gave breath to her emotion.

Words Hudson couldn't believe after she'd rejected any talk of God. She'd come a long way in a short period of time.

He dragged his eyes from her and turned to Benji's father. "Can you tell us what happened, Mr. Rossiter?"

"I was at work and got a call from the police. Benji had been found along with two teenagers at a halfway house. They were dead, but the police were rushing Benji to the hospital, so I got here as fast as I could." He pointed to his son, his lip quivering. "He's been like this ever since."

"Why do you think he was at this halfway house? I mean he has a good home with you, doesn't he?" Hudson took off his cap and set it on the bed.

David's eyes narrowed. "What are you insinuating?"

"Only trying to get answers as to why he was with those two teens doing drugs. I thought he stopped using."

David looked away. "Apparently, doda is a hard habit to break."

Kaylin rubbed Benji's arm as she spoke to David. "What did you do to him to make him start again?"

The man swore. "What are you talking about? I'm a loving father."

Kaylin turned to him and held his gaze. "He wanted out, so why did he start again?"

"I don't know. I raised my kids with everything. They didn't need to do drugs."

"You have other children?"

His eyes softened. "Yes, a daughter. Charlotte. She's eight. She's blind. Born with a genetic disease." He buried his head in his hands. "I can't lose Benji. This will kill her."

Hudson eyed Kaylin. Her contorted face registered pain. Was she thinking of her brother?

In a show of empathy, he squeezed David's shoulder. No matter his demeanor, the normally brash man loved his children. "I'm sorry."

Hudson's phone chimed with a text from his sister, Ally.

Matty is awake. He's asking for you.

Hudson pressed his palms to his suddenly stinging eyes and bowed his head, uttering a prayer of thanksgiving.

His nephew was going to be okay.

# FOURTEEN

Kaylin followed Hudson down the corridor of Windsor Regional Hospital toward his nephew's room. She sighed. A little too loud.

Hudson turned. "What's wrong?"

She stared into his eyes. Eyes that drew her like a fish to water. She couldn't escape his lure. Plus, being held by him earlier had solidified her feelings for him. There was no going back now.

But she had too much baggage. It could never work.

*He'll never be interested in you.*

She focused back on the case. "Why would anyone put a hit out on me on the dark web?"

"They're trying to get to your father through you. That's the only reason I can think of."

She threw her hands in the air. "Right about now, I'd believe anything because nothing makes sense about this case."

"And we're running out of time. Teenagers are dying. We need to stop this drug ring. Now." He directed her to Matthew's room. They nodded to the police officer stationed outside the door before entering.

The teen lay on the bed attached to an IV. His rumpled nut-brown hair stuck out in all directions, creating an amusing display. When he saw them enter, he tried to pat it down but to no avail. A weak smile formed on his ashen face. "Hi, Uncle Hudson."

Hudson rushed to his side, leaned down and gave him

a bear hug. "I'm so glad you're awake, Matty. How are you feeling?"

"Groggy. Weak."

"But blessed to be alive." Hudson's sister rose from the chair on the opposite side of the bed. "Praise God." She hugged Hudson. "Thanks for coming so quickly, brother."

He pointed to Kaylin. "This is Kaylin Poirier of the CBSA. Kaylin, my sister, Ally, and my nephew, Matthew."

Kaylin stepped forward. "So nice to meet you both." She shook hands with Ally.

"I've heard a lot about you." A lopsided grin formed on Ally's pretty face as she stole a look at Hudson.

Kaylin surmised it was probably about the last case they had worked on. "None of it good, I suppose."

"Hardly. My brother sings your praises." She winked at him.

Really?

Hudson cleared his throat and pulled up a chair close to Matthew's bed. "You wanted to see me? Can you tell me what happened?"

Tears welled in the teen's blue eyes.

Kaylin's breath hitched. Eyes just like his uncle's.

Hudson squeezed his arm. "Take it slow, Matty."

"Uncle Hudson, I want you to know I don't do drugs," he whispered. "The kids at school started pestering me into selling, telling me I'd get rich, but I kept saying no."

"Who tried to get you to sell?"

"Benji Rossiter."

Hudson glanced at her.

She noted the tightness in his jaw, the vein protruding on his neck.

"What happened? They're saying you overdosed." Hudson took out his notebook.

Matthew licked his chapped lips. "Benji forced me to

come to a meet. I didn't know what it was about until it was too late."

Kaylin stepped closer. "A meet with who?"

"The man didn't tell me his name, but I told him I wasn't interested. When he wasn't looking, I snapped a picture of him with my phone." He turned his head toward his mom.

She nodded and he continued.

"The next thing I knew, I felt a poke. I thought I'd been stung by a bee. I didn't know it was a needle. The man must have come up behind me." He rubbed his arm where the IV needle was now inserted. "A half hour later, I felt funny in my math class. Thought I was going to puke. Didn't know where I was. That was the last thing I remember."

"Do you still have the picture of this man?" Hudson asked.

Matthew reached his arm out. "Mom, hand me my phone."

She pulled it out of her purse and gave it to him. "You need rest, son."

"I will. I need to show Uncle Hudson." He put in his password and swiped through to the pictures. Then held it up. "This is him."

A bearded man in his midthirties, with dark hair and sunglasses on, appeared on the screen.

Kaylin hissed in a ragged breath. This man looked familiar. Could he be Valentino? Blaine?

"Send it to me and we'll put him through facial recognition." Hudson stood. "You did good, Matty. Now you need to rest."

His cell phone chimed and he read a text. He turned to Kaylin. "Mrs. Oliver passed away, but Mr. Oliver is awake. Time to go see him."

Hudson said his goodbyes and told Matthew he'd be back when he could.

His silence and furrowed brow told her he was concerned for his nephew's safety.

She touched Hudson's arm as the elevator climbed floors. "He'll be okay. God's got this." The statement rolled out of her mouth so easily now. Did she finally believe it?

He pursed his lips. "I know. I just hate that teens are being pushed to sell drugs. We need to put a stop to it."

"My father will see to it." And she would, too. She'd gladly put her life in jeopardy if it meant stopping drug smugglers. It was part of her job. Stepping into the line of fire.

The doors opened and they rushed down the corridor to the room where Lyle Oliver was. Kaylin knocked.

"Come in," a faint voice said.

She stepped inside with Hudson at her heels.

The florist was sitting up in his bed but was hooked up to an IV and heart monitor. His eyes widened at the sight of them.

"Mr. Oliver, how are you feeling?" Kaylin sat beside him.

"How do you think?" His voice was still raspy from the smoke he'd inhaled. "What do you want?"

Hudson stood on the other side of the bed. "Your shop was set on fire. What kind of trouble are you in?"

Lyle's eyes darkened. "My wife just died and you ask me that? How dare you."

Kaylin had to convince him they were on his side. "We're very sorry for your loss, but don't you want to help us find out who did this?"

He sipped his water. "I suppose, but I don't know anything."

Hudson crossed his arms. "Don't lie to us. We found

your ledger and all the shipment transactions. What were you involved in?"

Lyle cussed. "You don't understand. He'll kill me. The fire proved that." His softened voice revealed his fear.

Hudson inched forward. "Who? We can protect you."

"Not from him, you can't."

"Who is he?" Hudson asked.

"Blaine Ridley, but he's not the big boss."

"Valentino's the boss?"

Lyle nodded.

Kaylin grabbed his hand. "Give us the truth. Was your wife in on this, too?"

Tears formed in the man's tired eyes. "We did everything together."

"Tell us about your operation." Kaylin released his hand. "How did you do it?"

He crumpled the bed sheet, gripping it tight. "Blaine contacted us to see if we would ship dried poppies in our bouquets. Said the reward would be worth the risk of getting caught."

"How much did they offer?"

"Two hundred thousand per shipment."

Hudson whistled. "And you were able to get the necessary papers to get it across the border. How did you do that so easily?"

"We had someone on the inside forging the phyto-sanitary certificates."

No wonder they'd evaded getting caught until now. They had help from the Department of Agriculture. Kaylin needed to get her boss in on this right away. "Can you give us names?"

"Nope. Blaine arranged for all of it. Said the less we knew the better."

Hudson looked visibly disappointed but continued the

questioning. "What did you do after you received the shipment? Your ledger has you handing them off a week after they came in."

"We hung them in the back to complete the drying process."

Kaylin began a text to her boss as she asked, "Who did you hand them off to?"

"Blaine's men."

"Where did they take them?" Hudson asked.

He shrugged. "Don't know. Don't care."

Kaylin stopped texting. "You don't care that this drug is out on the streets because of the help you gave the smugglers? Teenagers are dying."

Lyle stared out the window. "Not my fault. I didn't push it on them."

Hudson scowled. "Anything else you can tell us?"

He fidgeted with the blanket wrapped around him. "That's all I know. Be careful."

"Why do you say that?" Kaylin finished her text and sent it off to her boss to get started with the Department of Agriculture.

"Because Valentino's tentacles reach far and wide. If he knows you're onto him, you're dead. Mark my words." More tears formed in his eyes. "He killed my wife."

Hudson pulled out his phone and held it in front of Lyle. "One more question. Do you recognize this man?"

Lyle's eyes widened. "Yes, that's Blaine."

Hudson turned the phone in Kaylin's direction to show her the picture Matthew had supplied.

At least they now had a positive ID.


"We've identified Blaine Ridley through a photo my nephew took. Mr. Oliver confirmed his identity." Hudson spoke to his boss on his cell phone outside the hospital room. "Now we need to catch him. He'll lead us to Valentino."

"We need a smoking gun," Miller said. "Something tying him together with this gang."

"Agreed. Any word on the shell casing found near the pier?"

His boss swore. "Not yet. Bianca is working hard at it, though. Listen, I'll be out of the office for the rest of the day. If you need anything, call Bianca. I won't be available."

"Everything okay?"

"None of your concern. Stay on track." He clicked off, the forceful tone in his voice telling Hudson his boss was definitely hiding something.

But what?

He clamped his mouth shut. No, his boss probably just had a medical appointment. That was all. But why did Hudson's instincts tell him something different?

His eyes followed Kaylin to the nurses station. Her shoulders slumped and she rubbed her head. Not good. Her earlier accident was beginning to take its toll on her. He needed to get her home soon. He checked his watch. Two o'clock. Would she consider a late dinner if she rested for a few hours? He didn't want his time with her to end for the day. Or was that selfish of him?

He shoved the phone back into his pocket and approached Kaylin. "Hey, you need to rest for a bit. You look tired."

"But I want to keep going. Talk out the case so we might get some ideas of who's behind this."

"How about I take you home for a rest and pick you up at six? We could go for dinner."

Her eyes widened. "You mean a date?"

He hesitated. Did she want it to be a date? Did he? Yes, but it couldn't be. "A chance to talk over the case. Dot our i's and cross our t's. Maybe we'll come across something we're missing."

"A tête-à-tête."

"Exactly. I've been wanting to try out that restaurant on Ouellette Avenue."

She nodded. "The Bunker?"

"You've heard of it? It's supposed to be awesome."

"My coworkers say it is. Sure, sounds like a plan to me."

He cupped his hand on her elbow, liking how it felt to be so close to her. "Let's go. To your place or Diane's?"

"Mine, but can we get Sassme from Diane's on the way?"

After picking up her cat and taking her home, he returned to the station to finish the day's paperwork and turn in his cruiser. Then he jumped into his Honda CRV and headed toward Kaylin's apartment. He'd returned home for a few minutes and taken a shower and changed into navy dress pants, a white shirt and a dark jacket. He hoped he wasn't too dressed up, but he wanted to look nice for Kaylin.

Would she notice or even care? Sure, they'd had a moment down on the beach, but how did she feel toward him? Did she consider him a friend?

The thought hit him hard. He wanted more. No doubt about it.

*Remember Rebecca.*

Memories of his ex's betrayal flooded his mind. The moment he caught her having a cozy dinner with another man, he knew she had deceived him. It wasn't until he found out she was cheating on him with two men that he realized the depth of it.

Was Kaylin like Rebecca?

No, he refused to believe it.

But he'd been wrong once before. Surely a cop could see through a woman's deceit?

He shook his head, trying to remove any further

thoughts of Rebecca and Kaylin. Tonight was about the case. Not a date.

At least that was what he told himself.

Hudson parked in front of Kaylin's apartment building and exited his vehicle. He punched the buzzer beside Kaylin's name on the apartment listing in the lobby.

"Hey there."

His heart played leapfrog at the sound of her voice. He breathed in deeply to slow it down. "I'm here."

"Be right there."

He tapped his toe, leaning on the railing. He had to calm himself, but the thought of seeing her again made the hairs on his arms dance.

Where was this excitement coming from? he asked himself. But he had no answer.

The door opened and Kaylin stepped through.

His jaw dropped.

She wore a white sundress with red flowers and dropped shoulders. The bottom scooped up in the front, stopping at her knees.

His heart jackknifed to his throat and words escaped him. He played with his keys to occupy his mind and shake off his momentary lapse.

"Hey there, Constable."

His pulse jump-started again.

She looked even more beautiful than she usually did.

He shoved his hands into his pockets. *Come on, Hudson. Use your words.* "You…you look lovely." Man, now she would think him a stuttering fool.

"And you, fine sir, look dashing. Shall we?"

He opened the passenger-side door. "Your chariot awaits."

She giggled like a schoolgirl.

A sound he loved.

Ten minutes later, they walked into The Bunker. The

darkened establishment played Michael Bublé and over-flowed with patrons sitting at their tables under candlelight. Good thing he'd made reservations. The place was bustling. He approached the hostess. "Dinner for two under Steeves."

"Good evening, Mr. Steeves." She grabbed two menus. "Right this way."

They followed her among rows of tables and booths strategically placed to offer privacy, but close enough to get a good crowd in the dining room.

The hostess walked to a booth in the corner. "Here you go. Enjoy your dinner."

"Thanks so much." He gestured for Kaylin to sit. Her lilac-scented perfume tickled his nose and he breathed in. He loved the freshness.

*Hudson, remember why you're here. The case.*

Right. He opened his menu and peeked over the top.

Her hair fell in soft curls past her shoulders. He imagined himself scooping it up and burying his nose in it. He could get lost there.

She looked up from her menu and raised her brow. "What?"

Busted. He glanced back down. "Nothing. See anything you like? My treat."

"You don't have to do that. I can pay my own way."

"Not after the day you had. I want to. Think of it as a celebration of coming to God."

Her smile lit up her face, suffusing it with a delightful beauty.

Wow.

The waitress approached, interrupting his thoughts of Kaylin. "Can I get you both a drink?"

"I'll have an iced tea, please," Kaylin said.

"Me, too."

The waitress named off the specials and left.

Kaylin set her menu down and pointed. "I like the sound of their rainbow trout."

"I think I'll stick to land and get their Angus beef."

"Funny." She closed her menu. "So tell me how you got into law enforcement."

"I met an officer while I worked at the shelter one day. He told me how he helped the homeless by trying to get crime off the streets. He wanted to keep them safe. His story resonated with me, so I enrolled that fall."

"You have a heart for the homeless?" Her eyes sparkled in the candlelight.

"I do, and that's where I met my best friend, Layke. He and I were on dish duty at the mission and we hit it off."

"He lives in Windsor?"

"Calgary. He's also a constable."

The waitress appeared with their drinks and they placed their orders.

Hudson took Kaylin's hand. "I wanted to tell you that you're making a difference at the CBSA."

She pulled away. "That's not how my father sees it. I need to solve this case and prove to him I'm a capable officer."

Sounded to him like she needed to prove it to herself first. How could he get across to her that she was worth so much more than just her job, that she had to believe in herself? "You're made in God's image and He's perfect."

She twisted her face. "I'm far from it. You don't know what I've done in my life."

"Tell me."

She looked away. "I can't," she whispered.

"Why?"

"Because you'll abandon me like everyone else in my life."

What was she referring to? Surely it couldn't be that bad. Once again, he grabbed her hand. "Look at me, Kaylin."

She shook her head.

"Please."

She turned her gaze back to his.

"I would never do that to you. You've wiggled your way into my heart." Did he just admit that out loud? "I want us to get to know each other better. Could you—"

"Hudson, there you are." A shrill voice interrupted their conversation. One he remembered.

Rebecca.

Kaylin narrowed her eyes at the interruption, her stomach churning. The beautiful redhead wore a designer coral dress with stilettos and wormed her way onto the bench next to Hudson. Kaylin recoiled, releasing her hand from Hudson's grip.

The woman stuck out her manicured hand. "I'm Rebecca. Hudson's fiancée. You are?"

Hudson squirmed. "You're not my fiancée."

She kissed his cheek, leaving a bright coral set of lips next to his mouth. She turned back to Kaylin and smirked, still holding out her hand.

She was stunning.

*I can't compete with her.*

Like she had a chance with Hudson anyway. He'd never go for her after he knew the truth. She lifted her chin and shook Rebecca's hand. "I'm Kaylin. I work with Hudson."

"Good to hear. I wouldn't want any woman moving in on my territory."

Hudson shook his head. "That's enough, Rebecca. Can you leave?"

"But I just got here."

He wiped the lipstick away with his napkin. "How did you know where to find me?"

She tsked at him. "I'll never give away my secrets. I

want you back in my life." She ran her long neon-orange nail across his chin. "We're meant for each other."

Awkward. Kaylin studied the centerpiece. Anything to get out of this moment. The woman had nerve—that was evident.

Hudson nudged Rebecca toward the edge of the seat, gently elbowing her off. "I'll never get back with you. You proved your true self when you cheated on me with two men."

Her chin quivered. "That's in the past, darling. I've changed."

"I don't care. Leave, or I'll have the owner throw you out." Hudson's nostrils flared as his darkened eyes held the woman's gaze.

She stomped away, heels clicking on the hardwood floor.

He slid back onto the bench. "Sorry about that."

"She's sure determined to get you back. You don't have any feelings for her?" Kaylin held her breath as she awaited his reply.

"Hardly. Besides, I have better people in my life now." He winked.

She exhaled. Could he mean he wanted more than friendship?

Impossible. She knew his philosophy on anyone holding secrets. He'd never forgive her after he found out the truth.

Time to change the subject and forget about any possibility of romance with him. "We need to discuss the case."

His brows furrowed as he leaned back in his seat.

Had she offended him?

She couldn't help it. She had to guard her heart. He chipped away at her armor and she had to stop it. Now.

She pulled her notebook from her purse and flipped to a page with questions on it. "First, we have Akio telling us about Blaine, whom we can't find. Percy confirmed

Blaine was Valentino's right-hand man and Matthew provided us with a photo of him. Lyle told us someone within the Department of Agriculture in the States is helping them get the flowers across the border. Seems this ring is bigger than we thought. We don't know who Valentino is, but he's the head of the gang."

"Yes, and he's targeted you and your father."

The waitress brought their meals and Kaylin unwrapped her silverware from the linen napkin. She breathed in the trout's scent. Her mouth watered.

She grabbed her fork. "We know he has gangs across the country and into Michigan. Why hasn't anyone sold him out yet?"

"They're scared of him. He's proved his ruthlessness and they abide by all his commands. Plus, he seems to have eyes and ears everywhere."

He took her hands in his. "Let's say grace, shall we?"

Right. Grace. How could she have forgotten about her newfound Father? She bowed her head and let Hudson take the lead.

"Father, thank You for this night and time together. I praise You once again for keeping Kaylin safe. Be with us now as we discuss the case. Give us insight, so we can bring these smugglers to justice." He paused. "Thank You for this food and bless it to our body's use. Amen."

"Amen." She reluctantly let go of his hands.

He grabbed his phone and punched in a number. "Let me check in and see if there's a ballistics report yet. Bianca told me she'd be working late."

Kaylin took a sip of iced tea and waited while Hudson spoke on his cell phone.

"What?" He sat up straighter. "When will we get the warrant?"

Muscles jumped under her skin. Did they just get a lead?

"Sounds good. The morning, then. Thanks again." He put his phone on the table. "Interesting news."

"What?"

"The police found a 51 mm shell casing near the beach where the sniper held his position before shooting Jake. The same slug was taken out of Akio. Both from an M24 sniper weapon."

"Same shooter in both cases, most likely."

"Looks that way. There's more."

She waited, praying it would lead them closer to the gang. "Tell me."

"They found fingerprints on the gas can used in the fire at DJ's Florist. Lyle Oliver's."

She dropped her fork. It clanked on her plate. "What? He torched his own shop?"

"Apparently. We got him on arson. He's being released from the hospital and we'll get the warrant in the morning."

"That's a big break."

He raised his iced tea. "To the possibility of an end to this case."

They clinked glasses.

Euphoric, she dug into her meal. A minute later, her cell phone buzzed.

She swiped to bring it alive. A picture of her and Hudson raising their glasses at the restaurant moments ago popped up on the screen.

Stop your investigation or you'll pay.

Kaylin dropped her phone and glanced around the room as an erratic pulse of terror swept through her veins.

*They're watching.*

# FIFTEEN

Kaylin's heartbeat crashed against her ears, pulsating quicker by every moment. She gripped the sides of the table and closed her eyes as nausea rose in her throat. Who was this person targeting her? She thought it had ended with Jake's death, but it appeared there was still a stalker out there. How did they get a number for a police-issued phone? It was clear. Someone had infiltrated the police.

She pushed her dish away. She'd lost her appetite. Her knife slipped from her plate and clattered to the floor.

"Kaylin, what's wrong?" The concern on Hudson's face melted her heart.

She turned the cell phone in his direction. "Look at this."

He picked up the phone, eyes widening. "I thought it was Jake who targeted you?"

"It appears I have more than one stalker."

He grabbed his phone. "We really need to contact your father. Get you off the case."

She placed her hand on top of his. "Please don't. He'll never let me hear the end of it."

"Don't you think he'll want to keep his daughter safe?"

"Probably, but I don't want to take the chance."

He raised a brow. "What aren't you telling me?"

How could she explain without him judging her?

*Trust.*

The word popped into her mind. Was God showing her what to do? If so, it was time to come clean. She looked him straight in the eyes. "Promise you won't hate me."

"What? I could never do that."

*Father, I need guidance. Should I share my secret? What if Hudson rejects me?*

God had led her out of the boathouse. He would help her now.

"You once said you couldn't trust anyone keeping secrets. Well, I've done that. There's much you don't know about me. A lot I've kept hidden from many people." She twisted her napkin as if trying to wring out past hurts.

He shoved his plate aside and took her hand. "Tell me, Kaylin. I listen well and I promise, I won't judge you. Not after the many mistakes I've made in my life."

She hesitated.

"Please. I can help." Hudson squeezed her hand. "What is it?"

"My father isn't what he appears to be." She held his gaze. "He hates me."

He tilted his head. "What do you mean?"

She pulled away. Could she go on? She had to. No turning back. "When I was born, my mother hemorrhaged and died. My father lost the love of his life and gained a colicky baby. One he grew to hate as the years went by."

Hudson drew forward. "How do you know that?"

She draped a cardigan around her shoulders, trying to keep out the drafts of the past. "Because he ridiculed me with every breath. I couldn't do anything right and, believe me, I tried."

"I'm so sorry. I find that hard to fathom. He seems so gentle. Caring."

"Looks can be deceiving. He did the same to my brother. After years of verbal abuse, Todd took up drugs." She tugged a strand of hair, curling it around her finger. "I lost the only hope I had when I was ten. My best friend."

Hudson rubbed her arm. "That must have been hard."

A tear rolled down her cheek, but she did nothing to stop it. "Very. It got worse after that."

He wiped her tear away with his thumb. "Did you try telling someone?"

She huffed out a heavy sigh. If only it had been that easy. "That was just it. No one would believe me. My father acted all innocent, putting on a pious face at church."

"That's why you found it so hard to trust God."

She fiddled with her pendant. "Yes, how could I accept Him as a Father after the example I had here on earth? No way."

"What did you do?"

"I couldn't take it anymore, so I stole money and ran away when I was fifteen." The best thing she'd ever done. Facing it had been hard, but she knew she had to do it. "But soon the money ran out and I ended up on the streets."

Hudson intertwined his fingers with hers. "Where you met Mary."

His touch calmed her racing heart.

Her lips curved into a smile. "Yes, she sheltered me from all the others who only wanted to hurt me. She introduced me to another young girl. Hannah. My best friend." The only ones who truly understood her. Would she be able to add Hudson to that list? Her pulse fluttered at the thought, but would he still want to be her friend after this confession? "We met Diane at the shelter. She felt sorry for us and took us in. Clothed and fed us. Gave us a roof over our heads. I now realize God put that loving, amazing woman in my path." Why hadn't she'd seen it before?

"But you and your father are talking now, right?" Hudson asked her.

She picked at her fingernails. "After seven months, my father found me and confessed he'd changed. Said he was sorry for everything and wanted me to come home."

"What did you do?"

She slumped back against the booth, blowing out a breath. "Diane convinced me to give him another chance, so I did."

"What happened?"

Somewhere in the restaurant, a diner scraped a chair. She jumped. Talk of her father always put her on edge even after all these years. "He was the gentle, loving father I had always wished for."

"So why do you still think he hates you? I don't understand."

How could she explain it when she had a hard time figuring it out herself? Her father tried hard to make amends after all these years, so why couldn't she let him? "It's me. I'm holding on to the past. Diane urges me all the time to forgive him, but I can't."

He took a drink. "She's right, you know. Bitterness will overtake you if you don't. Believe me, I know."

Did he have secrets, too? "Rebecca?"

He fiddled with a college ring on his right hand. "Yes. I need to forgive her, but also myself."

"What do you mean?"

"I, too, have secrets. Ones I've kept to myself for years." He paused.

She caressed his fingers. "Tell me."

"I lost a parent, as well. My father shot himself when I was eight years old."

"Oh, Hudson. I'm so sorry."

"I saw him do it." The vein in his neck protruded as if reliving the event.

"What?" The turmoil he must have gone through after witnessing such a horrific tragedy was evident. It was a wonder he'd turned into such an amazing man and not one living in fear. Then again, he had God on his side.

"Yes. The image has haunted me all my life. I blame myself for his death."

"But why? You didn't pull the trigger."

"That's what my mom told me, too, but I had just gone through a week of disobeying him and he had told me he was disappointed in me. I thought I wasn't a good enough boy and he didn't want to live anymore." He rubbed his stubbled hair.

"That's foolish."

Hudson took a sip of his iced tea before continuing. "I know, but that's all my eight-year-old brain could think of. I eventually had to forgive myself and years of counseling helped me see that."

"Did you forgive him?"

"I'm learning to. That's why I want you to try and do the same with your father."

She pulled away. "I wish it was that easy." Kaylin chewed the inside of her mouth. Should she tell him all her secrets? This one would definitely make him reject her. But she needed to get everything off her chest. She picked up her fork and played with her food, stalling the inevitable. She put the utensil back down.

*Get it over with, Kaylin.*

"There's more and I'm scared to tell you."

"Why?"

"Because of what you'll think of me."

He shook his head. "Whatever happened in your past is just that. The past."

"When I was younger and started to date Jake, I made some bad decisions. I wasn't a Christian and didn't know better. Diane warned me, but I still didn't listen." She hesitated. "I did drugs with him."

"Even after what happened to your brother?"

"I know. It was stupid and a bad judgment call, but I

wanted him to love me. I was scared if I didn't do what he said, he'd leave me." She hung her head.

He reached across the table and tipped her chin up. "Listen, we've all made bad decisions when we were younger. We grow from them."

"But you'd think I'd know better. I still can't believe I did it."

"For how long?"

"Couple of months. I came to Diane's place high one day and she was livid. She challenged me, knowing my background. Told me Jake wasn't worth it." She fiddled with her sweater. "I knew she was right and I had to break it off, so I mustered up the courage and did it."

"Good for you."

"But then a year ago, we got back together. He said he'd quit doing drugs. We got engaged. I found out later that he lied. After I learned he was selling drugs, I knew I needed to help put him away." It had been hard to let go of what she thought was love for him. Now she knew the truth. She just wanted someone to love her.

"And I came into the picture."

"Yes." She cradled her head in her hands. "Do you hate me now?"

He grabbed a hold of her wrists and pulled her hands from her face. "I couldn't hate you, Kaylin. You need to forgive yourself for your mistakes."

Tears welled. "I know. I feel so unworthy."

"God has forgiven you. Why can't you do the same and believe in yourself?"

She shook her head. "I don't know."

"God will show you how."

"Thanks for listening and being so understanding."

"Anything for you."

Their gaze locked and the moment stretched on while

the clinking of dishes and glasses sounded around them. Her heart hitched. Did that mean he cared for her? Wanted to be more than friends, even after everything she'd shared?

First, they had to solve the case. Nothing could happen before.

He pushed her plate back toward her. "Shall we eat now?"

"Of course. Sorry for the interruption."

"You don't have to apologize. I'm glad you finally told me." He cut into his steak and took a bite.

By the time they finished their dinner, she was exhausted. She rubbed her eyes and yawned. After an overwhelming day, her weary body demanded sleep. Especially after nearly dying today.

"You ready to head out? We have another big day tomorrow." Hudson grabbed her hand and stood. "Stay close to me in case we're still being watched."

She did a cursory check of the room, but there were only diners enjoying their meals. Or so it seemed.

Fifteen minutes later, Hudson pulled his car to the curb in front of her apartment building. They walked up the steps to the door in silence.

The stars twinkled in the summer night. She breathed in and let out a soft whoosh of air. Peace settled into her body as her limbs relaxed.

*Everything is going to be okay.*

He turned her to face him. "Kaylin, I want you to know I respect you even more for telling me your story."

"Thank you for being so understanding. You're an amazing guy."

He traced her face with his finger and stepped closer.

All around her, crickets chirped like a syncopated orchestra.

Hudson eyed her mouth, moving in slowly.

Then stopped and pulled back.

Was he thinking about Rebecca? Maybe he wasn't over her.

She stiffened. Even though he respected her for telling him about her past, he only wanted to be friends. Perhaps he was right. They had a job to do and romance wasn't in the picture. "See you tomorrow."

That night she tossed and turned as dreams of kidnappings, drownings and her father held her captive. No matter what she did, she couldn't shake the recurring pictures rolling by in her slumber world.

It was a fitful, restless night and she didn't fall asleep till nearly daybreak.

Her cell phone beeped, waking her early in the morning. She fumbled for the device and held it to her ear. "Hello?" Her voice sounded foggy from lack of sleep.

"Kaylin? Help me. I'm—"

She jolted upright. "Daddy? What's wrong?"

Silence.

"Daddy!"

She heard another voice come onto the line. "We told you there'd be consequences if you didn't listen. Now your father will pay."

The menacing voice sent a chill racking her entire body.

*Lord, protect my father. I need to tell him I love him. Before it's too late.*

Hudson sipped his coffee as he waited for Kaylin. He thought about their evening together. Why had he pulled back last night at her door? *You know why.* His heart couldn't take another rejection, especially since his feelings for this woman had grown. He found himself thinking about her when she wasn't around and his heart thumped while they were together. He had to contain his feelings. It would never work between them.

Lyle Oliver had been released from the hospital and arrested late last night after the judge signed the warrant earlier than expected. He now waited in the interrogation room.

The office door slammed open and Kaylin rushed toward him, her eyes wild and hair disheveled.

He rose from his chair. "Kaylin, what's wrong?"

"They have him. We need to find him. Before they kill him." Her breathless words came out forced.

He pulled her toward a chair. "Sit. Slow down. Who has who?"

She plunked herself beside him. "The stalker has my dad."

"What? When did they call?"

"Half hour ago. I raced to get here. We need to see if Bianca can get a hit from the number or do whatever you guys do." She shoved her cell phone across his desk as tears slipped down her cheeks. "I need to tell him I love him. Before it's too late."

"I'll take it to Bianca right now." He wiped her tears with his thumb. "We'll find him."

She wrapped her arms around her stomach. "I hope so."

He rubbed her shoulder, then pulled away. He had to stop getting so close to her. It wasn't the right time. "Stay here."

He explained the situation to Bianca. She downloaded information from Kaylin's phone and handed it back, promising to do all she could to help. In the meantime, they had to interrogate Lyle. He walked back to his desk.

"Bianca is checking into it." He handed Kaylin her cell phone. "We have Lyle Oliver. Let's talk to him. Maybe he has information that could lead us to your father."

She popped out of the chair. "Yes, let's go."

His cell phone dinged and he checked the text. No. He drew in a rough breath. "Bad news. Benji Rossiter just died."

Her shoulders slumped. "What a waste."

"Agreed." He sent up a prayer for the family. *Thank You, Lord, that Matthew is okay.* He had to find whoever was killing these teens. They had to be stopped.

He nudged her toward the interrogation room and opened the door. "After you."

He sat at the metal table across from the florist.

A five o'clock shadow had formed on Lyle Oliver's normally clean-shaven face. His shoulders drooped as he scrunched his body forward. Clearly, he knew he was in trouble. How much would he share willingly? They wanted Valentino, so maybe they could reach a deal.

Hudson threw the florist's journal on the table. "You're more involved than you let on."

The man grimaced. "No comment."

Hudson pulled out a recording device and turned it on, stating the time and date along with the names of those present. "You have the right to an attorney. Do you want to make a call?"

"Don't need one. I'm innocent."

Kaylin harumphed. "We've got you on arson. You set your own shop on fire, so you might as well come clean on everything. We've stopped the flow of goods from coming across the border. It's over."

He sat upright, eyes narrowing. "I did not set the fire." His lip quivered. "I would never put my wife in danger."

Hudson opened the journal. "I looked closer at your entries earlier this morning and checked your financials. You said they paid you two hundred thousand per shipment, so why does your bank account show five hundred thousand per entry in the past few months? Can you explain that?"

Kaylin gripped the sides of the table and leaned into the florist, getting into his personal space. "And what have you done with my father?"

His eyes bulged behind his round-rimmed glasses. "What are you talking about? I don't know your father."

"The police chief. You kidnapped him."

"And when do you think I would have done that? I was just released from the hospital last night and then arrested."

Good point, Hudson thought. He had them there.

"Why the increase in funds?" he asked, going back to his original question. Maybe they could follow the money trail.

Lyle slouched in his chair, releasing a long breath. "It was getting harder and harder to get the flowers across the border. We were putting our business on the line, so we asked for more money."

"And they just gave it to you?" Hudson asked.

"My wife could be very convincing."

"Why not grow the poppies here?" Kaylin sat and made a note.

"We tried, but the bigwig said the soil wasn't quite right."

"I find that hard to believe," Hudson said.

"A dealer in Michigan said they already had a crop growing and for a good price, he'd sell it. The boss agreed."

"Give us the names of your person inside the Department of Agriculture and the individual growing the poppy." Kaylin shoved her notebook and pen across to him. "And stop lying to us. You had to know in order for your driver to get the shipments across the border."

He wrote names down and handed it back to her.

Hudson closed the journal. "After you received the shipments, where did you refine the poppy into doda?"

"At a warehouse here in Windsor. We shipped it throughout all of Canada after we were done."

So the man did know more than he'd told them. "Give us the location."

He named the address and Hudson wrote it down. They needed to check on it and perhaps catch them in the act. An idea formed and he held up the key Chief Harrison had found in the remains of the florist fire. "Will this give us access to the warehouse?"

Lyle nodded.

"Tell us who Valentino is," Kaylin told him.

Lyle pounded his hand against his leg. "I already said. I don't know."

Kaylin leaned forward. "So, you worked for the man but never met him? How did you conduct business?"

"How many times do I have to explain? Through Blaine Ridley."

Hudson bolted upright, chair scraping on the floor. "Do you know where he's hiding?"

"No idea."

"Can you help us set up a sting with Valentino?" Hudson hoped this was their chance to get the man. "We need to stop his organization."

"Only Ridley knows how to get in touch with him."

"How can we contact Ridley?"

"He's gone dark. I tried a couple of days ago."

Hudson stood and picked up the journal. "We're done here. Call your lawyer. You're going to need him. Someone will be by to book you."

Hudson strode out of the room with Kaylin close behind.

Kaylin tugged at her tousled hair. "We don't know where my dad is."

"We need to find Ridley. He's the key."

She pulled out her phone. "I'll call my boss to get US Homeland Security involved with the arrest of the accomplices in Michigan."

"Sounds good. I'll check with Bianca to see if they found anything on your cell phone."

She nodded and walked away.

Hudson punched in Bianca's number. "You find anything on Kaylin's cell phone that will help us find her father?"

"Dead end, I'm afraid. We've put a BOLO out on him. The entire police force is combing the city."

He walked toward his desk. Not good. Kaylin was already worried enough. How could he help? "Anything more on the autopsies?"

"I should know in about an hour. I'll call when I find out. You get any leads from Oliver?"

"The name and address of a warehouse where they do the refining. Heading there as soon as we get a warrant." He reeled off the information.

"One more thing, and I hate to bring this up," Bianca said.

Hudson bristled. "What?"

"We checked Lyle Oliver's cell phone records and one number kept popping up."

"Whose?"

A pause. She sighed. "Miller's."

Hudson stopped. No. It couldn't be. "Are you sure?"

"Yes. Watch your back." She hung up.

What could Miller be involved in? Perhaps it was only a coincidence, but Hudson didn't believe in those. His boss was holding out on them.

Hudson spent the next few minutes on the phone with the judge, explaining the situation regarding the warehouse. Thankfully, the judge agreed to draw up a warrant within the hour. Fastest he'd ever seen one issued. Of course the police chief's abduction helped expedite it.

Kaylin returned, shoving her phone in her pocket. "Done. My boss is on it. Actually seemed pleased about the find."

"Maybe you're in someone's good books now."

"Hopefully." She pointed to the door. "Time to check the warehouse. They may have Dad there."

He pulled her back. "First I need to tell you something." He explained the information Bianca had shared.

"Do you think Sergeant Miller is dirty?"

"I'd call him a lot of things, but not sure I'd ever suspect him as a dirty cop."

She rubbed the back of her neck. "What do we do?"

"Be on guard. For now, we'll pick up the warrant on the way and I'll contact Miller to get a team assembled to check it out. Pray there's a reasonable explanation for all this." He fished his keys from his pocket. "This is a good lead. Maybe we can finally shut this ring down."

"We still don't know who Valentino is."

"We will."

An hour later, after picking up the warrant and calling his boss, Hudson pulled into the parking lot at the warehouse with a team behind him. They inched their way to the entrance, weapons drawn.

"Everyone, keep your heads up. This place could be crawling with people not wanting to be caught. Expect anything." Hudson pulled out the key and inserted it into the lock. The door opened, squeaking in annoyance.

His eyes adjusted to the dim lighting. Tables lined the large storage area. Dried poppy straw hung from the rafters. Equipment to crush the poppy into powder lay on every table. Bags of the drug were piled in boxes.

This was definitely their operation.

But where were the workers?

Cigarette butts smoldered in ashtrays, leading him to believe they'd left in a hurry.

Had someone tipped them off? How had they known they were coming?

Hudson removed his hat and wiped his forehead. The only answer he could come up with was that someone within the police department was working against them. Miller?

He straightened. No, he refused to believe it. "Span out, everyone. Check the back offices for people. Looks like everyone abandoned this place, but there could be some hiding. Be careful." He bent to look in the boxes, when a flashing red light under the table caught his eye.

He exploded upright. "Bomb! Everyone out!"

He grabbed Kaylin's arm and ran. Others followed.

*Lord, protect us. Get everyone to safety in time.*

They rushed out into the parking lot, trying to get as far back as they could, when an explosion rocked the building and sent them sprawling.

Hudson slammed into the pavement with Kaylin beside him, as debris rained down upon them.

He scrambled on top of Kaylin.

He had to protect the woman he loved.

# SIXTEEN

Buzzing assaulted Kaylin's ears as Hudson's weight smothered her. She struggled to catch a breath in the dusty debris and wheezed. "Hudson, move. Can't breathe."

He rolled off her and sat up. "Are you hurt?"

She eased into a seated position, holding her stomach. Did they really just get bombed again? Who did this and how did they know they'd be there?

"Kaylin, talk to me."

Dust permeated the area, coating everyone's clothing and skin. Wreckage from the bomb detonation littered the parking lot. Pieces of the building lay in chunks around them. How had they escaped unharmed? Only one answer she could think of. God.

She rubbed her scraped arms. Blood oozed out of the cuts. Her knees throbbed from the impact with the pavement. In. Out. In. Out. Her breathing finally regulated. "Just got the wind knocked out of me. You okay?"

"I'm good other than scrapes and bruises."

She massaged her neck. "God protected us. If you hadn't bent down to check those boxes, we would've gone up with the building."

Hudson stood and wiped the dust from his arms, leaving a smudged mess. "Everyone okay?" His voice boomed across the parking lot.

The other officers waved to show they were fine.

He called 911 to ask for EMS and firefighters.

Not that there was anything left to salvage. The building lay in rubbles. No way they'd be collecting evidence now. Someone had succeeded in destroying it.

"Hudson, how did they know we were coming?"

He scratched his head, his lips tightening. "Someone on the force tipped them off."

"How can we trust anyone?" She rubbed her eyes and squeezed the bridge of her nose.

He brushed off his pants. "We can't. Everyone is a suspect now."

They needed to solve this together, without the help of others.

His cell phone rang. "Hey, Bianca. What do you have for me?" He kicked at stones around him. "I see. Okay, thanks."

Hudson's face hardened, his eyes narrowing.

She grabbed his arm. "What is it?"

"The tox report on the two teenagers who OD'd came back. There was a high dosage of fentanyl in both victims' systems along with the doda. Plus some in Matthew's system."

Kaylin whistled. "You mean they're lacing the doda with fentanyl?"

"No wonder it killed those kids. They didn't have a chance. Obviously, there wasn't enough in Matthew's body to kill him. Praise the Lord." He pointed to the rubble. "And now we can't find the drugs. They're buried."

"Maybe we can salvage something."

Hudson shook his head. "Doubtful."

"So what do we do?"

"We take down the kingpin and then the business will crumble."

She threw her hands in the air. "But how? We don't know who he is."

"We need to find Blaine and your dad."

Kaylin's phone rang. It was her boss. "Hey, Superintendent Thompkins. What's up?"

"I got in touch with Homeland Security and they've detained two men at their border you need to talk to."

"Who?"

"One from the Department of Agriculture and the other a poppy grower. Can you and Constable Steeves head over to the Detroit border?"

Firefighters arrived and entered the building while EMS workers checked on the police officers. "Will do. We just have to wait to have this situation contained here."

"What happened?"

She updated her boss on the bombing and her father's abduction.

"You okay?"

"Yes, sir. Will keep you updated."

"Stay safe. We'll find him."

Her boss actually sounded like he cared. He seemed to have turned a corner when it came to her. She hoped it was true.

A text sailed into her cell phone.

I'm watching you. Did u really think you'd catch me?

A video popped up on her screen.

Her father bound and gagged. A masked man behind him with a knife to his throat.

Her breath hitched. *No!* "Hudson!" She shoved her phone in his face and pressed Play.

"Your father will pay for threatening our drug family," a distorted voice hissed through her phone. "This is your final warning or you will also die."

Marshall Poirier struggled in the chair, his voice muffled behind his gag. The video ended.

"No!" Kaylin dropped to her knees as her pulse thundered in her head. A rush of tears sluiced down her cheeks.

Hudson knelt and pulled her into his arms. "Lord, protect the chief. Lead us to where they have him."

Would God hear Hudson's prayer or let her father die? Before she had a chance to tell him she forgave him?

Should she quit the investigation? Let it go? A past conversation between her and her father bubbled to the surface of her mind.

"You see every case to the end, you hear me? No matter what." Her father's determined voice rang through her ears. It was something he'd told her when she'd started at the CBSA.

He wouldn't want her to stop now. Even if it meant his life.

She backed away from Hudson's embrace and stood. "I have to find him and that means finding Blaine. My boss just called with a lead, but we have to go to Detroit and see Homeland Security."

His blue eyes softened as he stood. He took her hand. "We'll find him. Let me call Miller and let him know."

"Are you sure we can trust him?"

"No, but I don't have a choice."

Two hours later, after they finished with the bombing scene and the EMS bandaged a cut on her arm, they crossed the Ambassador Bridge. The busiest border crossing in North America saw thousands of trucks and cars cross from the US and Canada each day. They pulled up to the booth and explained the situation. The security officer waved them through and they parked in front of the building.

The darkened skies threatened to explode at any minute, but they couldn't let it impede their investigation. The forecast hadn't mentioned a thunderstorm. However, in these parts the weather could turn in a flash. The low-lying clouds promised a doozy at any moment. Kaylin trembled and pulled her collar up closer to her neck. She hated storms and liked to hide under the bed like her cat, Sassme. She shook off her fears and opened the car door.

A balding man in his early forties waited by the entrance and stuck out his hand. "Officer Poirier, I assume. I'm Officer Roger McCosh of Homeland Security."

Kaylin shook his hand. "This is Constable Hudson Steeves. We're working on this case together."

"Welcome. We have the gentlemen quarantined in separate rooms waiting for you." He opened the door and guided them in. "The officers who arrested them said they put up a battle."

Hudson frowned. "I'm not surprised. They're facing serious charges."

"We're happy to help in any way we can," Roger said. "We heard this ring has invaded the Detroit area."

"Yes, we're trying to bring it down." Kaylin said. "Once we do, we'll know how far it reaches."

He grabbed a file from his desk and gestured toward a closed door. "Let's start with Cabe Collins. Thirty-three years old. Works at the Department of Agriculture."

Roger opened the door and they stepped inside.

A brawny African American man sat tall in his chair. Kaylin refrained herself from staring. He obviously pumped iron to be so huge. No way would she want to meet him in a dark alley.

Roger introduced them as they sat. "They're here to ask you questions about this doda ring."

The man placed his hands behind his head, leaning back. "Don't know anything."

Roger handed Kaylin the file. "We'll be the judge of that."

Kaylin opened it and stared at the man's dossier. His

record included armed robbery and drug trafficking. "How did you get a job at the Department of Agriculture with a record like this?"

"Let's just say I was good at faking IDs. They never suspected a thing."

They were fortunate Lyle had given them his real name or he probably would have gotten away with it. She shoved the file toward Hudson.

He opened it. "Tell us what you did to help get the poppy straw across the border."

"I ain't saying anything without a lawyer present."

"You really want to play that card? A man is about to be killed. We could charge you with accessory to murder."

The man's eyes darted back and forth. "Fine. The florist would contact me every time he knew a load was coming across and I'd get the certificates ready for the driver. He'd pick up the shipment from the grower and stop by to see me. I'd give them the paperwork and they were all set. End of story."

Kaylin folded her arms across her chest. "You left out the part where teenagers are dying because of this new enhanced doda."

His eyes widened. "What are you talking about?"

Hudson leaned forward. "The doda is mixed with a lethal dose of fentanyl."

He put his hands in the air. "Hey, man, I didn't have any part in that mess."

Roger stood. "You did and you're going to pay for it."

Hudson shifted in his chair and steepled his fingers. "Anything else you can tell us? Do you know the name Valentino?"

"Nope. Just dealt with the florist and Blaine."

Kaylin leaned back. "Blaine Ridley?"

"That's him."

Kaylin eyed Hudson.

He lifted his brow and stood. "How can we get in touch with Mr. Ridley?"

"You can't. He always contacted me through the dark web." His lips formed into a twisted grin.

Another dead end. Kaylin pushed away the desire to wipe the smug look off his face, but stood instead. "We're done here."

"What about me?" Cabe towered over them.

Roger shoved him back into the chair. "The police will be by shortly to take you to jail. You won't be issuing any more certificates."

They closed the door behind them.

Kaylin scowled. "Every story leads back to Blaine."

"Yup. I'll guess this other guy will tell us the same thing."

They questioned the poppy straw grower, but didn't get anything further from him. Same MO and Blaine's name came up again. He was definitely the key, but how could they unlock this mess? Did Blaine have her father?

Kaylin and Hudson thanked Roger for his help and left the Detroit border, making their way across the Ambassador Bridge during the rush hour traffic. She turned up the air conditioner. The heat stifled her just like her frustration with this case. "Do you think we'll ever get a break on Ridley's whereabouts? He must be the one who has Dad."

Fat rain drops splatted on the windshield. One. Two. Three.

Kaylin peeked at the skies. The clouds were about to open.

"We're out of leads. Let's broaden the area and include Detroit in the search. Maybe he fled into the States."

"But how did he get across the border?"

Hudson shrugged. His cell phone rang and he hit

the talk button on his console to activate the bluetooth. "Steeves here."

The rain fell in sheets now, pounding the car.

"Constable, help me." The faint voice sounded out of breath.

Golf-sized hail bounced off the hood.

Hudson turned the wipers on full force, but it wasn't enough to clear their view.

Kaylin straightened in her seat, gripping the armrest until her fingers turned white. "Who's this?"

They swerved to miss a car in front of them as it slowed.

"Blaine Ridley. He's after me."

Hudson jerked his head back. "Who?"

"Valentino."

Hudson strained to hear. The static on the line was too loud and the pummeling hail didn't help. "Where are you, Blaine?"

Could it be true? The person they needed to find the most had called them? God had sent a gift. Maybe they could locate the chief and have this wrapped up by the end of the day.

*Please, Lord. Make it so.*

"In a cabin outside of Windsor. Close to Amherstburg, off County Road 20."

Hudson turned on his siren and flashing lights, moving in and out of the bridge's traffic. "What markers can you give me? That's a good stretch of road."

Forked lightning flashed in the distance.

"There's a red mailbox at the end of the long driveway. The cabin is back in the woods. Hurry."

"How do you know Valentino is after you?" Hudson pushed on the accelerator.

"I have a friend who works closely with him. He tipped me off."

"How long ago?"

"Twenty minutes. You've got to hurry or I'm dead. Come alone. I don't trust anyone but you two."

Kaylin leaned forward. "Do you have my father?"

He clicked off.

Hudson swerved around a transport truck. The driver laid on the horn.

The cruiser fishtailed, hydroplaning on the wet pavement.

Kaylin grabbed the side of the door to steady herself until Hudson righted the vehicle. "This is the break we needed. It could lead us to Dad."

"I know. Valentino has a twenty-minute head start on us." Hudson's cell phone rang again. Bianca. He hit the button. "Talk to me, Bianca."

"Chief Harrison found remnants of the doda drug laced with fentanyl at the warehouse. Some were locked in a safe, so it survived the blast. And I did some checking and through some back channels I discovered the building was owned by Raison Industries."

Where had he heard that name before? He racked his brain trying to figure it out, but it lay hidden somewhere in the recesses of his mind like a lost piece to the puzzle.

"One other thing." Bianca interrupted his thought search. "We got a lead on Ridley. He was seen in Amherstburg."

"We know. He called and we're headed there now. Tell Miller, but we're going in alone. We don't want to scare Ridley."

"Can we trust Miller?"

Hudson tapped his thumb on the steering wheel. Could they? He didn't have a choice at this point. "We have to."

"There's a tornado warning out," Bianca told them. "Stay safe."

Hudson disconnected the call.

He honked at other cars to get them to move out of his way. They needed to cross the border and fast. He zipped in front of an SUV and sped through a law enforcement lane back into Canada, holding tight to the wheel. He headed toward County Road 20, picking up speed on the highway.

"Watch out!" Kaylin yelled, pointing to a slowing truck ahead of them.

He slammed the brakes on the slick highway and they lurched forward. At the last second, he swerved around the truck and right into oncoming traffic.

Kaylin yelled.

Hudson accelerated and pulled right, avoiding the cars just in time.

*Thank You, Lord. Keep us safe.*

He turned onto County Road 20, tires screeching at the sharp acceleration.

"Slow down or we'll never see the red mailbox." Kaylin clutched her seat belt. "The rain is making it impossible."

He eased up on the gas and looked right and left, watching for the landmark that would take them to the cabin. The wipers screeched out a rhythm as they fought to keep the windshield clear.

Ten minutes later, Kaylin pointed. "There!"

A red mailbox lay on its side.

Hudson took a sharp right turn onto the dirt road.

"Turn off your siren. We should approach with caution."

"Agreed." He flipped the switch, silencing the siren, and slowed down to enter the woods in stealth mode in case Valentino had already arrived.

Evergreen and pine trees lined the road, giving privacy

to the area. They rounded a bend and a log cabin came into view, with a porch wrapped along the side.

"Nice place to visit for another reason." Hudson crawled along the long driveway, looking in the woods for any signs of being watched. "It looks empty. Maybe we beat him here."

"I get the feeling Valentino knows how to hide. He's done it for how many years now?"

"Good point." He hit a rut in the dirt driveway, lodging the front tire deep and stopping their approach. He stepped on the gas, but the wheels only spun. Great. How would they make a quick getaway now? "We're stuck. Stay alert."

Hudson grabbed two Kevlar vests and raincoats from the trunk. "Put these on. I want us to take all precautions."

He checked the sky through the trees. Funnel clouds formed in the distance. *Lord, keep the tornado away from us.* Rain assaulted them, drenching them within seconds. Even the wooded area didn't shield them from the fierce weather.

They both unholstered their weapons and crouched low, approaching the cabin while keeping their eyes peeled in every direction. Other than the storm, everything appeared quiet, but Hudson knew all too well that anyone could be hiding. Waiting. Ready to attack.

He stepped onto the porch. It creaked. So much for stealth mode. He inched his way to the door with Kaylin behind him.

The door opened and a bearded man beckoned them inside. "Hurry."

They rushed through the door.

Blaine bolted it, pointing his gun at them. "Show me your credentials."

Hudson raised his hands. "Whoa now. You called

us, remember?" He pulled out his badge, flashing it in his face.

Kaylin did the same. "Where is my father?"

"What?" He stuffed his weapon into the back of his pants. "I don't have him."

"Give me your gun." Hudson stretched out his hand.

Blaine hesitated but gave him the weapon.

Hudson shoved it in his waistband. He shook the rain off his coat. "Now tell us the truth. Where is Marshall Poirier?"

The man gestured around the cabin. "Look around. I don't have him."

Kaylin rushed him, grabbing his collar. "Then where is he?"

"Probably with Valentino."

She released him.

Hudson surveyed the room and checked for every possible exit, in case they needed to get out in a hurry. The living room housed a couch with timber legs, giving it a rustic feel. A rocking chair sat in one corner. The fireplace was positioned in the middle of the far wall with a bearskin rug in front of it. Seemed as if this was the perfect hunter's oasis. "You own this place?"

"Yes. Bought it a year ago to get away from the city life and Valentino." He limped to the rocking chair and sat.

Kaylin eased herself down on the end of the couch.

Hudson took a position in the chair facing the door. "Tell us about your relationship with the man." They needed to wrap this up before the storm worsened.

"Will you give me immunity if I spill the beans on the drug ring?"

Could Hudson bargain for information? He'd have to check with the prosecutor, but Blaine wasn't the one they wanted. They needed to put Valentino behind bars. "Why should I help you? You tried to kill my nephew."

Blaine bit his lip, fidgeting with the button on his tight shirt. "I panicked when he wouldn't cooperate. But, man, you need me. Without my testimony, Valentino will get away with everything."

Hudson hissed out a sigh. The man was right. They needed his help. "I'll do my best. I promise."

"I want it in writing."

Hudson took out his cell phone and pressed Record. This was one interview he needed to tape. "Do you really want to go down for accessory to murder? Those teens died because of the drug you helped traffic. You'll be fortunate if you get a reduced sentence."

The man's knee bounced. "Fine. I'll take my chances and go on your word. What do you want to know?"

Kaylin stood and traced her fingers along the mantel. "How long have you been involved in this ring?"

"Five years."

"How did Valentino recruit you?" Hudson asked as he wrote notes on his pad.

"Through the dark web. I then brought in the Olivers. I know you have Lyle in custody, so he probably ratted on me."

Hudson snapped to attention. "How do you know that?"

"Let's just say we have someone on the inside."

Thunder shook the cabin and the wind howled as the branches slapped the windows.

"Who?" Hudson asked.

Blaine shrugged. "I don't have a name. I just know that this person has been helping spy for Valentino to keep him one step ahead of the police and CBSA."

Hudson clamped his hands together. He suspected his boss, but was it true? The man had served his country for years. What would have turned him into a dirty cop?

"So we know how you got the goods into the border, but how did you get it out again to the gang in the States?"

"You haven't figured that out yet? Thought you border patrol people were smart."

Kaylin erected her back and moved closer. "Tell us."

"We put the powder packages in crates along with household goods. Toasters, coffee makers, you name it." He chuckled. "No one was the wiser."

"How many gangs are there within the organization?" Hudson said.

"Five or six. Spread across the country, and one in Detroit." He smiled, showing his graying teeth.

Was he proud of what he'd done?

Hudson's face flushed. This man needed to be put away for his part in this. He hoped the prosecutor would not give him a deal. "Did you shoot Akio Lee and a man named Jake Shepherd? Did they send you to do their dirty work?"

Suddenly Blaine popped out of the rocker. "Come on. We gotta leave before he gets here."

"Sit down," Hudson said in a stern voice. "You're not going anywhere until we know the entire truth."

Blaine plunked himself back into the rocker. "What else do you want to know?"

"Did you or did you not kill those men?" Hudson was tired of this man's attitude.

"No! Valentino has a sniper at his disposal. I didn't do it. I swear."

Could he believe him? After all, he was a criminal.

Kaylin walked to the other side of the room and peered out the window. "Why did you try to kidnap me?"

"Only following boss's orders. Nothing personal." He rubbed his wounded leg.

The thought of what could have happened to Kaylin sent heat slamming through Hudson, but he pushed it aside.

For now. "Do you have proof of how big this drug ring is? Proof that will help us stop it and put them all away?"

He pulled out a flash drive. "Right here."

"What's on it?"

"Financials, buy-off videos, even footage of Valentino and the sniper he hired."

"Give it to me and we'll consider helping you get a reduced sentence." Hudson took it from Blaine's hand and pocketed it. "Why help us now?"

Blaine's mouth curled downward. "Valentino betrayed me. Put a hit out on me because I failed to capture your girl here." His gaze narrowed and turned to Kaylin.

Hudson's desire to protect her bubbled up again, bringing with it his previous feelings. "Get away from the window," he told her. "You never know—"

Glass cracked and a shot rang out from a distance, barely missing Kaylin. She dove to the floor and rolled, unholstering her weapon. Multiple bullets pelted the window, shattering it. Rain poured through.

"Get down!" Hudson yelled to Blaine. He raised his Smith & Wesson and hugged the wall, inching his head toward the window.

A figure skulked by the large oak tree in front of the cabin. How many more men were out there?

"Olly Olly Oxen Free." A voice boomed through a bullhorn. "Come out with your hands up."

Blaine raised his head. "That's Valentino."

"Kaylin, check the back door. See if you catch sight of any more men."

She made her way to the rear, crouching low. "I see two men behind the trees."

"I know you're in there, Constable Steeves and Officer Poirier. Give up your witness and I may let you live, especially if you want to save the chief's life."

Hudson admonished himself. He should have called for backup.

But he hadn't wanted to risk losing the witness. Too late for that now. He pulled out his cell phone to call the Amherstburg police. The closest help. He glanced at his screen.

No signal.

The storm must have taken out the cell towers.

*Great, now what do we do, Lord? Show me.*

They couldn't shoot their way out. It was too risky, and even though Kaylin was trained in weaponry, she wasn't a policewoman. His only hope was that Bianca had told Miller and they had a team en route to their location. Or was Miller part of this? He cringed at the thought.

"Time's up." Valentino's laugh sent a chill up Hudson's spine.

Would this be how Hudson died? In a shootout? He glanced at Kaylin. Her wide eyes revealed fear, and something else.

Did she feel it, too? He'd found her only to lose her to Valentino? Before Hudson had a chance to tell her how he felt?

He gripped his weapon tighter.

*Protect us, Lord.*

Another shot rang out, splintering the wooden door.

Hudson pointed his gun out the broken window and fired, while Kaylin broke the back window and got off two shots.

Gunfire peppered the side of the cabin.

They both hit the floor as the door burst open.

David Rossiter stepped into the cabin, his gun raised. He shoved a hooded man through the entrance. "Now you all die." He pulled the hood off.

Kaylin gasped.

"Daddy?"

# SEVENTEEN

Kaylin scrambled to her father and pulled him into her arms. Her heartbeat thrashed inside her head at the sight of his bruised and swollen face. She feathered her finger over his cheek. "Are you okay?"

He nodded. A tear slipped down his face. An abnormal action for the tenacious police chief.

Kaylin's muscles tensed as she gazed at the man who caused her father's pain.

David Rossiter was Valentino? She stared into his evil eyes and shuddered. One thought raced through her mind.

They were going to die.

He'd never let them go.

She glanced at Hudson, holding his gaze. Would she be able to tell him how she felt?

Or ask her father for his forgiveness? She realized now that she'd held on to her anger for too long.

She stood and inched her way over to Valentino. "How could you kill your own son?"

The man stiffened. "I never thought he would take the new stuff." He raised his gun higher, eyes determined. "Enough about me. Both of you, throw your weapons on the floor."

Kaylin dropped her gun and kicked it away from her.

Hudson rose to his feet, casting his weapon aside. "Wait. Now it fits together. You work for Raison Industries. I saw your portfolio at the hospital. I knew that sounded familiar when I heard Raison Industries owned the warehouse.

You funded your operation through your company. Why did you need more money? Are you that greedy?"

A man entered from the back of the cabin.

"Secure the prisoners," Valentino ordered him. He walked closer to Hudson. His eyes flashed. "I have my own reasons."

His spindly lackey secured Hudson's hands and shoved him into a chair. And then did the same to Blaine.

Hudson pulled at his restraints. "Why not tell us everything? You're going to kill us anyway."

"Fine. I told you about my daughter, Charlotte." His cold eyes softened.

Kaylin didn't miss the love for his child flash on his face. Wait—Charlotte was blind. From birth. It hit her. "You were paying for some kind of new treatment, weren't you?"

He blinked. "It was the only way."

"So you sacrificed one child for the other?"

He shoved his gun's barrel into her temple. "Don't you dare talk about my children."

"And now we all pay the price." Her lips curled upward. "You're a coward."

He slapped her across the cheek and shoved her into a chair, securing her hands behind her.

The blow stung, but she refused to show fear.

Her father stumbled to his feet. "Don't you touch my daughter."

Hudson struggled in his restraints. "Leave her alone."

Valentino marched over to where Hudson sat and shoved his gun to his heart. "How touching. Two men love you, Officer Poirier. How about I end their lives and let you watch? Your punishment for not staying out of my business."

Hudson raised his chin. "Go ahead. If you don't, I'll make you pay for hurting her."

Valentino pistol-whipped him in the head.

Hudson slumped forward.

Kaylin wobbled in her chair. "No! It's me you want."

Blaine whimpered. It was the first noise he'd made since Valentino had burst through the door. She'd almost forgotten his presence.

"Valentino, let me go," Blaine said. "It's these guys you want. I promise I won't rat on you. After all, I've been a diligent employee, doing your dirty work."

Valentino pointed the gun in Blaine's direction. "Shut up, you useless tool of a man. I know what you were going to do. Betray me. No one does that and gets away with it."

Blaine raised his hands. "I didn't. I'm faithful to the cause."

"Hardly." He pulled a walkie-talkie from his pocket. "Do it."

Who was he talking to? His sniper? Kaylin bristled. Who would they kill? She glanced at Hudson.

Their gaze met and he tilted his head, mouthing, "I'm sorry."

"This is what happens to people who betray me," Valentino said.

"Don't do it, Rossiter." Would she lose the man she loved? And her father, too?

Lightning flashed, illuminating the darkened skies. Then the lights flickered as a blast rang out, booming through the woods and into the cabin.

Blaine dropped. Shot in the temple. Blood pooled around his fallen body.

Assassin style. The same sniper who took out Akio and Jake.

"Who's out there?" Kaylin shouted at their captor.

"Something you haven't figured out yet."

"Why did you have Akio Lee and Jake killed? What did they do to you?"

Valentino sneered. "Akio was a liability. Collateral damage. Jake? He just got in the way. My sniper followed you and took him out."

"Tell us about your empire." Her father sat straighter. "When did it start?"

"Years ago, when I began working at Raison Industries. Management liked my ideas and soon promoted me. They gave me a raise, but I wanted more, so I started selling heroin. I rose to the top with my drug sales and began recruiting men to work under me."

"What other type of drugs did you sell?" Kaylin spotted her gun on the floor. Could she get to it before anyone noticed? She eyed the man standing guard at the exit. Too risky. She'd never get a shot off before he took her out.

"Cocaine, fentanyl. You name it."

"Why doda?" she asked.

"To add to my list of goods. There was a demand for it among the Asian community."

"But why lace it with fentanyl? You're killing teenagers. Doesn't it bother you to see teens die, especially your son?"

He shook his head. "Benji was stupid. He liked his drugs and just took too much at once."

"That's rich coming from you, a drug kingpin." Kaylin shimmied her hands, trying to once again loosen the ropes.

"Enough talk. Who do you want to die first?" He shoved the gun into her father's chest. "Your dear old dad?" He pointed to Hudson. "Or your boyfriend? You choose."

*Forgive your father.*

The thought raced through her mind like a whisper from God. Could she forgive him after all the hurt he had caused? She eyed the man before her. Yes, he had betrayed her all those years, but that didn't define her. Not anymore, since she'd become a Christian. Diane had told her that her Heavenly Father commanded them to forgive. Seventy times seven.

She sat upright. She wouldn't let bitterness consume her any longer. For what life she had left, she would be free. Free of guilt. She had to tell her father before it was too late. "Daddy, can you forgive me for hating you all these years?"

Marshall Poirier contorted his face. "Only if you can forgive me."

She nodded. "I do love you."

"Enough." Valentino rushed over and slapped her across the face. "Shut up."

Her lip stung as blood flowed down her chin. Iron filled her mouth and she spat it out. She would not kowtow to this man. She'd made her peace. Whatever happened next was up to her Heavenly Father. *God's got this.*

She knew Hudson would hate seeing her hurt, but she didn't expect his next move. Mustering all his strength and emitting a growl, he lunged out of the chair and headbutted the man standing next to him.

Kaylin took the opportunity and dove for her weapon, knowing it was her last chance. But Valentino reacted, kicking her hard in the ribs. She stumbled backward.

The lights went out again in the raging storm and the door burst open. She heard a voice shout, "Stand down. Both of you."

Kaylin halted in her tracks and Hudson froze as they looked at the intruder.

Bianca stood in the doorway, her sniper's gun pointed at them.

Hudson's jaw dropped and he wiggled his hands in the ropes, trying to free himself. To think the woman he worked with every day had sold them out. "Bianca? How could you?"

Her lip curled. "Why do you think? Money, of course."

Valentino laughed. "It was the perfect relationship. I paid her big bucks and she did my dirty work for me."

"How else do you think he was able to stay one step ahead of you?" Bianca asked. "I fed him information, all the while casting suspicion onto Miller. I put the hit out on Kaylin through the dark web. Kept feeding them her cell numbers. I also hired the nurse to take out Percy Brown." Bianca walked over to him and stuck her M24 rifle in Hudson's chest. "Don't move or I will shoot."

He stood his ground. "How could you betray your country?"

"Money talks."

Heat rose to his cheeks as anger threatened to bubble over. Why did he not suspect her? Was he that bad a cop? No, she was just that good at playing the game. Once again, he was duped by a female and this one would cost him his life. And Kaylin's, if he couldn't come up with a plan to save them all. He still had the flash drive in his pocket. Proof of Valentino's drug empire.

Would he live to show the world?

*Lord, give us both strength to fight this. Show me a way.*

He had to keep them talking, so he could think of a plan. "How did we not know you were a sniper?"

"Once Valentino recruited me, I took training in my spare time. He needed not only an informant but a sniper. I was up for the task."

He snarled. "You disgust me."

"Sit down." She shoved him back in the chair. Water dripped off her soaked coat, leaving a puddle on the floor. "Oh, by the way, the cavalry's not coming. Miller doesn't suspect a thing."

Great. He'd hoped his boss would be his saving grace. What now?

They were outnumbered and his hands were tied. And they were in a cabin in the middle of the woods.

Secluded.

In a storm.

He'd appeal to Bianca. It was their only chance.

He looked up at her. "Stop doing this. Help us bring Valentino down and end this madness. You've done so much good in helping us solve cases. Don't throw your career away."

"What makes you think I won't keep working with the forensic unit? Once you three are eliminated, no one will be the wiser."

She was going to kill them all.

Hudson turned to Valentino. "Why put more blood on your hands?"

"You don't get it, do you, Hudson?" Bianca waved the gun in his face. "He doesn't do the killing. I do. He just runs the business, brings in the money."

"Did you also bomb the warehouse and my cruiser? I know Lyle set the flower shop on fire."

She shook her head. "That's where you're wrong. I framed him. Put his fingerprints on the can. Clever of me, right? I also learned how to build bombs. I'm one smart girl."

"That's why I hired her." Valentino's evil laughed filled the room. "Lyle was getting greedy. We needed to get him out of the picture, so setting him up worked out well."

"You both make me sick," Hudson said. "One day you'll trip up and the cops will take you down."

Valentino shoved the gun into his belly. "I have too much power at Raison Industries. I've hidden my business this long."

"Do they know?"

"How do you think I moved up the ladder? They like

all the business I've done and now they're scared of me. They turn a blind eye."

Marshall shifted in his chair. "You'll never get away with this. Don't you think they'll come looking after they find the police chief, his daughter, who is a CBSA officer, and a police officer dead?"

"He's right. Lyle will help take you down," Hudson said. "We have him in custody."

Bianca laughed. "Not for long. He'll commit suicide. Sorrow over the loss of his precious wife. I will see to that."

Valentino sneered. "And after, she'll take out your nephew for getting in the way. And your sister. We need to prove to everyone that no one messes with the drug kingpin in this city."

"No! Leave them out of this." Hudson squirmed. Too many lives were at stake, but how could he stop Valentino's evil plan and save those he loved?

He needed to overtake one of them and grab a gun.

It was their only chance.

He joggled his fingers, trying to free the ropes from his wrists. This time they loosened.

Almost there.

He caught Kaylin's eye and tilted his head toward Valentino. She must stall him. Create a diversion so Hudson could act. Would she get his meaning?

One more minute and his hands would be free. He twisted hard, the rope cutting into him. He ignored the pain. Finally, he wiggled out of them but kept his hands behind his back to give the illusion he was still tied up.

Kaylin cleared her throat. "David, don't do this. Let us go. We'll help you get the assistance you need for your daughter. I promise."

He turned and hauled her out of the chair. "Like you'll really do that. Nice try."

Kaylin shoved him—hard—and he stumbled back.

That was Hudson's cue.

He leaped out of his chair and plowed into Bianca, knocking the gun from her hands.

Marshall threw himself toward Valentino's henchman, but he raised his gun.

Before he could pull the trigger, a shot fired and the gunman dropped.

"Valentino. Bianca. You're surrounded." Sergeant Miller's voice boomed through the bullhorn.

The cavalry was here. How, Hudson didn't know, but he was thankful.

He grabbed Bianca's rifle from the floor and aimed it at her. "Stay there."

Once more Kaylin charged at Valentino. They collided, the gun falling from his grip.

Peter Miller, followed by a handful of other officers, rushed through the splintered door. "Police! Stand down."

Bianca raised her hands, but, undaunted, Valentino shoved Kaylin aside and stood. "You'll never take me alive."

He pulled a gun from the back of his pants and raised it toward Kaylin.

Hudson dove in front of her as the shot boomed, the sound resonating throughout the small cabin.

His neck burned like a bee sting. His hand flew to his wound, and he felt blood oozing through his fingers.

He struggled to stay upright as a deafening sound echoed around them. A train rumbling the cabin.

No, it was a tornado swirling around them.

*Lord, save us.*

Though he called out to his Father, darkness called out to him.

He fought it, but it was too powerful.

He crumpled to the floor.

* * *

"No!" Kaylin scrambled for the gun in the corner.

Valentino raised his weapon once again, his finger moving on the trigger. His intense gaze revealed his intentions.

He would kill them. She needed to act before it was too late.

She took aim and fired.

A bullet slammed into Valentino's chest.

He snapped his gaze her way and she saw something flash in his eyes. Regret? Perhaps only for a second.

He clutched his heart and collapsed, his lifeless eyes staring up at the ceiling.

The tornado tore the porch off the front of the cabin. The wood flew in different directions.

Tears coursed down her cheeks. Tears for Hudson. Tears for her father. Tears for herself.

They'd survived Valentino, but now the storm would take them all. There was nowhere to run.

She slid to the floor.

Her father scrambled to her, pulling her into his arms. "I'm so sorry, Pumpkin. I love you."

"I love you, too, Daddy." Years of regret coursed through her veins and then a wave of peace washed over her. The same peace she'd felt in the boathouse. God's peace.

It was all she needed.

Her father rocked her as she sobbed, holding her tight. She drew in a forced breath, waiting for the end.

And then—

Silence.

The tornado slithered around the cabin, then left them unharmed.

"Kaylin?" Hudson's whisper beckoned to her. He'd come back to consciousness.

She rushed to his side and examined his body. The bullet had grazed his neck, just above the Kevlar vest. She hugged him. "Thank you for saving me. You didn't leave me."

"Never." He caressed her cheek. "Valentino?"

"I shot him. He's dead." Her lip quivered. She could hardly believe she'd killed a man.

"I'm so sorry you had to do that."

"He would have killed us all." Of that, she was certain. "The tornado passed us by."

"God is good." He looked around the cabin. "How's the chief?"

Her father patted his shoulder. "I'm right here, Steeves. Thank you for saving my daughter."

Sergeant Miller cleared his throat. "I'm glad you're all okay. You had us worried."

Hudson eased himself up, still clutching Kaylin. "How did you know where to find us?"

"We followed Bianca."

"But how did you know about her? She fooled me." Hudson's face contorted. "She made me believe it was you."

"I began to suspect someone at our station was feeding Valentino information. There were too many coincidences. That's why I was so secretive. I couldn't trust anyone, so I did some investigating on my own. I narrowed it down to her and when I couldn't get a hold of you, I knew something was wrong. We tailed her and she led us here." He walked over and poked her shoulder. "You're going down for murder."

She snarled. "You can't prove it."

Hudson pulled the flash drive out of his pocket. "Yes, we can. Everything is on this. Blaine paid with his life to get it to us."

Miller grabbed her arm and cuffed Bianca. "You're done."

Kaylin jumped up. "Wait, there's another man outside."

"We got him. He's restrained in the back of our cruiser. The scene is secure. I'll go radio for an ambulance. If the tornado left my cruiser out there. Sit tight. Chief, help me with this one?" Together they hauled Bianca out the door, leaving Kaylin and Hudson alone.

With three bodies.

She sent up a prayer of thanks that they'd come out of this alive.

Then she heard Hudson moan and remembered his injury.

Racing back to his side, she pulled him into a hug. "Stay with me. An ambulance will be here soon."

"I'm not leaving you. Ever."

What was he saying? Did he really want a relationship with her? Even after everything she'd shared with him?

He touched her cheek. "You're beautiful."

"And you're delirious."

"I'm more in focus than I've ever been." His gaze locked with hers, his eyes dancing. "Will you be my girl?"

She smiled. Could she trust another man? This man?

She didn't have to decide long. She knew her answer. "Yes."

He leaned in, eyeing her lips.

She inched closer. She swallowed the lump in her throat, anticipation overtaking her entire being.

When he kissed her, her heart fluttered.

The sun broke through the darkened clouds, beaming into the cabin.

Time stood still and a thought wedged in her mind. *God is good. All the time.*

*Four months later*

Kaylin sat on the park bench next to the pier. Not that far from where Hudson had saved her life. She marveled at all God had done for her in such a short time. He'd not only given her a new start, but an amazing man to share it with. And a renewed relationship with her father. The waves crashed against the shoreline, reminding her of God's peace.

She smiled. God had given her forgiveness in her heart. Now only peace remained.

She volunteered along with Hudson at the local mission. She knew within her heart it was what God wanted her to do. After all, He'd kept her safe on the streets and she wanted to give back to the community. Perhaps even help keep kids from turning to drugs. It was the least she could do after all she'd learned.

David Rossiter's daughter had taken her father's death hard and sobbed at the funeral. After all, she'd lost both her brother and dad. All in one swoop. Charlotte now lived with her aunt. Kaylin vowed to help Charlotte wherever she could. She wouldn't let the young girl pay for her father's sins.

Bianca was charged with multiple first-degree murders and sentenced to life imprisonment. They had shut down the drug ring across the country and Michigan. The evidence on the flash drive had helped bring it to its knees.

Hudson had healed from his wound and was back solving crimes. His nephew, having recovered, had vowed to help other teens stay away from drugs. Just like his uncle.

Right now, Hudson sat beside her. His stillness was comforting. He put his arm around her and pulled her closer.

She leaned into him, laying her head on his shoulder. It was the only place she wanted to be.

Birds chirped nearby and the fresh autumn breeze

flowed through her hair. She breathed in the welcome smell of fallen leaves. "I love this time of year."

"Me, too." He reached behind him and pulled something from his work briefcase.

He stood and turned toward her, holding out a fresh bouquet of flowers. Not deadly ones like they'd confiscated at the border, but gerbera daisies arranged with yellow roses. Her favorite.

"They're beautiful." She brought them to her nose, taking in their sweet scent. "You're the best."

He reached into his pocket and bent on one knee, bringing out a small box.

"Kaylin Poirier, I love you with all my heart. Will you marry me?"

She sprang up from the bench, hauling him up with her. "Yes!"

She wrapped her arms around him. "I love you, too, Hudson Steeves."

He brought her closer, their soft kiss sealing the deal.

Yes, God had given her not only her life back but an amazing man to share it with.

Her forever love.

* * * * *

*Uncover the truth in thrilling stories of faith in the face of crime from Love Inspired Suspense.*

*Look for six new releases every month, available wherever Love Inspired Suspense books and ebooks are sold.*

*Find more great reads at www.LoveInspired.com*

Dear Reader,

I hope you enjoyed reading Kaylin and Hudson's story as much as I loved crafting it. It was fun to create their world and delve into their lives. Living in Canada, I've always been fascinated by Canadian law enforcement and the Canada Border Services Agency. I knew I needed to write them both into a story because they often work together. Plus, who doesn't love a handsome constable?

I felt it was important to give them everyday struggles because it's reality, right? There are times we need to move forward and forgive so we don't become bitter. It makes us stronger.

I'd love to hear from you. You can contact me through my website www.darlenelturner.com and also sign up for my newsletter, to receive exclusive subscriber giveaways. Thanks for reading my story.

God bless,
*Darlene L. Turner*

**WE HOPE YOU ENJOYED
THIS BOOK FROM**

# LOVE INSPIRED SUSPENSE
## INSPIRATIONAL ROMANCE

*Courage. Danger. Faith.*

Find strength and determination in stories
of faith and love in the face of danger.

**6 NEW BOOKS AVAILABLE EVERY MONTH!**

LISHALO2020

# COMING NEXT MONTH FROM
## Love Inspired Suspense

### Available May 5, 2020

## CHASING SECRETS
*True Blue K-9 Unit: Brooklyn* • by Heather Woodhaven

When Karenna Pressley stumbles on a man trying to drown her best friend,
he turns his sights on her—and she barely escapes. Now Karenna's the
only person who can identify the attacker, but can her ex-boyfriend, Officer
Raymond Morrow, and his K-9 partner keep her alive?

## WITNESS PROTECTION UNRAVELLED
*Protected Identities* • by Maggie K. Black

Living in witness protection won't stop Travis Stone from protecting two
orphaned children whose grandmother was just attacked. But when his
former partner, Detective Jessica Eddington, arrives to convince him to help
bring down the group that sent him into hiding, agreeing to the mission could
put them all at risk.

## UNDERCOVER THREAT
by Sharon Dunn

Forced to jump ship when her cover's blown, DEA agent Grace Young's
rescued from criminals and raging waters by her ex-husband, Coast Guard
swimmer Dakota Young. Now they must go back undercover as a married
couple to take down the drug ring, but can they live to finish the assignment?

## ALASKAN MOUNTAIN MURDER
by Sarah Varland

After her aunt disappears on a mountain trail, single mom Cassie Hawkins
returns to Alaska...and becomes a target. With both her life and her child's
on the line, Cassie needs help. And relying on Jake Stone—her son's secret
father—is the only way they'll survive.

## HOSTAGE RESCUE
by Lisa Harris

A hike turns deadly when two armed men take Gwen Ryland's brother
hostage and shove her from a cliff. Now with Caden O'Callaghan, a former
army ranger from her past, by her side, Gwen needs to figure out what the
men want in time to save her brother...and herself.

## UNTRACEABLE EVIDENCE
by Sharee Stover

It's undercover ATF agent Randee Jareau's job to make sure the
government's 3-D printed "ghost gun" doesn't fall into the wrong hands. So
when someone goes after scientist Ace Steele, she must protect him...before
she loses the undetectable weapon *and* its creator.

**LOOK FOR THESE AND OTHER LOVE INSPIRED BOOKS WHEREVER
BOOKS ARE SOLD, INCLUDING MOST BOOKSTORES, SUPERMARKETS,
DISCOUNT STORES AND DRUGSTORES.**

LISCNM0420

# Get 4 FREE REWARDS!

### We'll send you 2 FREE Books
<u>plus</u> 2 FREE Mystery Gifts.

**Love Inspired Suspense** books showcase how courage and optimism unite in stories of faith and love in the face of danger.

FREE Value Over $20

---

**YES!** Please send me 2 FREE Love Inspired Suspense novels and my 2 FREE mystery gifts (gifts are worth about $10 retail). After receiving them, if I don't wish to receive any more books, I can return the shipping statement marked "cancel." If I don't cancel, I will receive 6 brand-new novels every month and be billed just $5.24 each for the regular-print edition or $5.99 each for the larger-print edition in the U.S., or $5.74 each for the regular-print edition or $6.24 each for the larger-print edition in Canada. That's a savings of at least 13% off the cover price. It's quite a bargain! Shipping and handling is just 50¢ per book in the U.S. and $1.25 per book in Canada.* I understand that accepting the 2 free books and gifts places me under no obligation to buy anything. I can always return a shipment and cancel at any time. The free books and gifts are mine to keep no matter what I decide.

Choose one: ☐ **Love Inspired Suspense Regular-Print** (153/353 IDN GNWN)  ☐ **Love Inspired Suspense Larger-Print** (107/307 IDN GNWN)

Name (please print)

Address                                                                  Apt. #

City                              State/Province                Zip/Postal Code

### Mail to the **Reader Service:**
**IN U.S.A.:** P.O. Box 1341, Buffalo, NY 14240-8531
**IN CANADA:** P.O. Box 603, Fort Erie, Ontario L2A 5X3

Want to try 2 free books from another series! Call 1-800-873-8635 or visit www.ReaderService.com.

*Terms and prices subject to change without notice. Prices do not include sales taxes, which will be charged (if applicable) based on your state or country of residence. Canadian residents will be charged applicable taxes. Offer not valid in Quebec. This offer is limited to one order per household. Books received may not be as shown. Not valid for current subscribers to Love Inspired Suspense books. All orders subject to approval. Credit or debit balances in a customer's account(s) may be offset by any other outstanding balance owed by or to the customer. Please allow 4 to 6 weeks for delivery. Offer available while quantities last.

**Your Privacy**—The Reader Service is committed to protecting your privacy. Our Privacy Policy is available online at www.ReaderService.com or upon request from the Reader Service. We make a portion of our mailing list available to reputable third parties that offer products we believe may interest you. If you prefer that we not exchange your name with third parties, or if you wish to clarify or modify your communication preferences, please visit us at www.ReaderService.com/consumerschoice or write to us at Reader Service Preference Service, P.O. Box 9062, Buffalo, NY 14240-9062. Include your complete name and address.

LIS20R